Aliens At Expom

Mike Hughes

C2C Publications

Aliens At Expom

BY

Mike Hughes

ISBN:0-9664130-6-7

Other Books by Mike Hughes:

The Northwest Dive Guide
Harbour Publishing Copyright 2009

The North American Dive Guide
Copyright 2012

Best of Intentions
Copyright 2012

To Kill A Diver
Copyright 1998 Printed 2013

Whoops Airlines Enhanced
Copyright 1998 Printed 2014

Whoops Diver's Guide Enhanced
Copyright 1999 Printed 2014

This is a fictional story about Aliens marooned on the moon. All names and people are not based on actual living persons. The actual events do not happen in our future timeline as best as I can tell, but could come to fruition in another time line.

This Book is dedicated to my mother,
Sandra Joy Adams

Prologue

Thomas Jefferson, an old man of African decent with mostly gray hair, was sitting in an old worn out chair that he couldn't get two bucks for if he sold it at the flee market. He was slowly rocking back and forth as he looked out the window of the two-room apartment. A small black and white portable television was sat on a nearby end table, but he didn't give it much attention. His grandson would be coming by to visit soon. He watched as people older than himself walked by. He watched as kids played in the street. He even watched as a young man not too different from his grandson give a local thuggee some green cash in exchange for a bag with white substance inside. It was a typical day for this section of Detroit. You won't see Kid Rock coming down this far south of the city and you wouldn't expect to see Eminem singing on a nearby street corner either. No one came down here unless they were forced to live here. Rent was cheap here sixty years ago and just as cheap now as it was back then. Thomas made sure that that would always be the case. He saw his grandson walking towards the apartment it was cold outside and his grandson wore a full length black wool coat buttoned up tight and sported a black knitted hat on his head. The other brothers walking these streets didn't dress as well, but they all left his grandson alone. His grandson, Jason, smiled and waved through the window then knocked on the apartment door.

"Come on in Jason." He opened the door, stepped inside, and gave his grandfather a big hug.

"How are you doing Grandpa?"

"Just fine Jason. You have any problem finding the place?"

"No Grandpa. Dad drove by here a couple of times when we was kids. He said you own it." Jackson nodded in agreement.

"Did he tell you that your grandmother and I lived here when we first got married?"

"Yes he did Grandpa."

"Well have a seat." Jason took off his coat and hat and sat down on a vinyl couch that was straight out of the 1950's. He knew that his grandpa was rich, so he never really understood why he kept the old furniture.

"I left this place looking just the way it did before your dad was born. Just to remind me of the past and who I really was, not what all the business people think I am." Jason looked around.

"That's cool, Grandpa." Jason folded his arms and sat with his back leaning forward as if ready to go the first chance he got.

"I brought you here to give you something." Jackson said.

"Grandpa, if it's about college, Dad has me covered."

"No, this is about something far more important than college." Now Jason was wondering what was up, because all he ever heard his grandfather talk about was going to college.

"Jason, I hear you've been having some dreams." He looked at his grandfather with a blank expression and then he suddenly connected.

"Oh, you mean my idea for a fiction book."

"I guess that's what I mean. Have you discussed it with your dad?"

"No, he says that if it has anything to do with space, the moon, or aliens, he doesn't want to hear about it."

"That's your dad.   He wanted to be a fireman since the age of five. I could barely get him to read unless it was a picture book on fire engines. I could have sent him to college, but he would have just flunked out. But then again, making 80,000 a year as a fireman pays more than lot's of college degree jobs."

"Yeah, dad loves his job, and he's not looking forward to retirement."

"No one does if they love what they do for a living. That's why I still work." Jackson stood up and walked over to a cabinet hutch.

"But that's not why I asked you to stop by." Jackson opened the cabinet and pulled out what looked like an old worn out shoe box only slightly wider and not so tall.

"I have something to give to you, that is if you want it." Jackson opened the lid and Jason could immediately smell the lingering odor of burnt paper. Jackson pulled out from the box a thick yellow bundle of typewriter size paper.

"What is it Grandpa?"

"This is a book manuscript that I've been saving for quite some time." He handed it to his grandson.

Jason held the manuscript and scrutinized the top page. Besides the yellow old appearance Jason saw brown burn marks. At the bottom of the page was printed "Page 23" the rest of the page read as the beginning of a new chapter in a book whose beginning pages were missing.

"Don't read it now. I want you to take it home with you. After you've read through it maybe we can talk about it. Jason wanted to read it right that minute.

"I didn't know you were a writer Grandpa."

"I'm not. I'll tell you all about the history of this manuscript, but only after you've read it. Can you do that for me?" Jason wondered why his grandfather was acting so strangely.

"No problem Grandpa, I'll start on the way home."

"In that case Jason, I best see you to the door." Jason stood and placed the manuscript back in the box." His grandfather put his hand on Jason's shoulder.

"I've got a lot things that I want to tell you, but they will only make sense after you've read the manuscript. And there's no point telling your dad about this. He already has enough on his plate. This is just between me and you."

"Not a problem grandpa." He wondered why his grandfather was so serious about it.

"It might be, once you've read the book." He held the door open as Jason left with the box tucked under his arm. As soon as Jason was no more than a few blocks away, his curiosity got the best of him and he opened the box and began to read the text on the old burnt and faded paper.

Page 23

A rush of fire enveloped my body as a category five hurricane whipped around me then, as if as an after thought, knocked me down on the ground. I woke to the sensation of burning skin. A roaring sound permeated my inner ears. With time, the ringing noise would subside from a thumping low-pitched drumbeat into the medium pitched ring tone, but never completely going away. The noise was tolerable, but the pain radiating on my outer extremities was too great to bear and kept me from rolling over in bed to see where I was. I knew I was in a hospital. I had to be. That would explain the dreams of nurses and doctors. I thought I heard one say that my prognosis didn't look good. I thought I heard the phone ring and wondered how that was possible because of the roar of noise already hammered so loud inside my head. The burning pain suddenly disappeared. In the dark with my head lightly wrapped with gauze, I reached over and answered the phone.

A soft "Hello" was all I could cough up.

"Hello John, this is Dan." Dan was my immediate boss and I don't know why I knew this.

"Hi Dan." I sat up in bed and tried to collect my thoughts.

"I hear your recovery is coming along just fine."

"Yeah?" I didn't know what to say. I didn't how I was just able to raise up. Light was now filtering into the room. I looked over at his nightstand and saw a handwritten note. The gauze over my head and eyes must have been part of my dream. It was weird how lifelike some dreams could be and you didn't know how real they felt until you woke up to dismiss them.

"Listen, take all the time you need, but give us a call the moment you decide to come back."

"Will do Dan," I heard the click at the other end of the line as I read the note:

Dear John,
Thanks for everything.
See you at Expom.
Andrea

The note had no date on it and I wasn't sure if it was placed there last night or if it had been sitting there for weeks. Next to the note was a brown pill bottle half empty and a brochure with a photo of the moon and the word "Expom" written in big bold font. Part of me recognized the brochure, but part of me had no memory as to what it meant or how it came to be in my possession. I laid back down and closed my eyes. Perhaps a little more rest and then it would all make sense to me.

Page 24

Standing in the great auditorium, I looked around to see if I recognized any of the other passengers. The auditorium was a refurbished wide body aircraft hangar. Several had been renovated here at Flagstaff air force base, which now served as the shuttle terminal to and from Expom. I was impressed by the mural depicting early space flight especially the moon landing module that separated from the main capsule and curved down towards the moons surface as a two piece unit. As I walked across the room, I half expected moon dust, or regolith, to swirl around my feet. Some unknown music softly played in the background to help sooth the passengers who were anxious to begin their journey into lower orbit. At the other end of the auditorium refreshments along with sandwiches were being served.

Abruptly a woman holding a microphone stepped towards the center of the great room and spoke up.

"Can I have your attention? Please?" Her voice was soft and sweet light that of a singer and everyone became quiet as they turned to see whom it was.

"Thank you. Please make sure that your boarding cards are correct, and that you have completed the quarantine documentation."

She then repeated this in Russian and Mandarin Chinese.

During this time I looked around to see how many nationalities had come together for this adventure. No matter what country they were from, I could tell that some of them had a far away look in their eyes as if they were still planning what they would do every second of their trip. Others seemed already bored. They were the ones just going so they could return and be the first to tell their neighbors and coworkers what the moon was really like. Or why Expom was a greater experience than any cruise ships their friends had ever been on, back on Earth.

Near the door to an adjoining room I could see a couple of people sitting in wheel chairs. They, along with other medical patients, were going to Expom for yet another reason. Apart from being know as the greatest tourist attraction currently known to

10

mankind, Expom also had one of the most advanced medical facilities. The fact of the matter was that with the reduced gravity pull, made arduously long elective surgeries less risky and patients recovered quicker than their water planet based counter parts.

Most of the passengers going to the medical section of Expom I would not see, for somewhere close by their shuttle *Eagle* was a sister ship that carried the more seriously ill passengers. I had read that the medical center was the only medical facility on the moon, but it would have ranked the best state of the art facility had it been built on Earth.

The lady finished her speech and the crowd began to mingle around the snack bar. I heard a low humming noise and turned around to see a mural being raised and exposing a passenger-boarding ramp similar to the jetways used at airports. The removal of the mural also exposed a large window through which passengers could view the last minute preparations before launch. Men and women wearing bright orange vests were busy loading the cargo-hold of the *Eagle*. An endless array of pipes and hoses lay between their feet, but not once did I see the tangled web of cables and hose interfere with their speed of performance. I noticed that I wasn't the only one amazed by the agility of the workers and the complexity of their tasks. A group of Japanese businessmen excitedly said out loud. "Scotchie, Scotchie," as they all pointed in unison in the direction of a large container marked "Galley 2". A flap of the container was slightly pulled back and a box marked "Scotch" could clearly be seen. The party would soon be relocated from the glitzy neon illuminated GINZA district of Tokyo to a more remote, sunspot-amplified site on the moon.

Over the intercom system came a very seductive voice, which informed the passengers of when they were assigned to board the *Eagle*. The *Eagle*, although enlarged, was designed to replicate the earlier space exploration vehicles and to give a more authentic retro spacecraft appearance right down to the simulated individual ceramic tiles covering the outside of the space craft hull. From the images I had seen, the inside of the ship was one of the most luxuriously equipped cruisers on the market. The ship could accommodate up to two hundred and ninety passengers traveling in a first class setting.

As the passengers passed through the entrance and up the

jetway ramp, two small hooded rats sitting on a counter sniffed for signs of weapons and controlled substances. One of the rats seemed to be in a playful mood and ran across the counter looking for a way to jump off and mingle with the guests at the snack bar. The other rat stood on its hind legs with its nose pointing forwards and sniffing at the wind. At about the same time the playful rat was ready to jump off the counter, one of the security guards grabbed the rodent and quickly shoved him into his coat pocket. Within seconds the half-dazed rat was sticking his head out of the pocket and once again sniffing the surrounding air. As I walked past the rats, I noticed a small probe barely visible on the tops of their heads. The probe was designed to transmit a pleasurable sensation after the rats had smelled narcotics or a host of other chemical concoctions. Past the living detectors, I stood on the ramp and looked down the length towards the head of the huge ship held tightly in its moonrail cradle. I hesitated, as my eyes followed the track until it veered upwards from the horizon. Along the length there were evenly spaced junction boxes presumably anti-gravity or reverse magnetic relay junctions. It all looked well maintained. I then walked inside the ship carrying nothing but my boarding pass.

"Good Afternoon Dr. Wilson," an attractive brunette said to me. She was dressed in a tight fitting gold colored Expom uniform with the familiar shuttle wings embroidered on her upper left chest region. The embroidered patch consisted of a small lunar globe in the center of two out stretched wings. The words *Inflight Representative* were written just above the wings. She looked very stunning even without the wings.

"Your seat is on the second deck. Please use the stairs at the cross aisle." She pointed and I headed over in the indicated direction. I soon sat down in a comfortably soft black leather chair. A parabolic monitor was imbedded in the seat in front of me. A list of instructions was printed on the right side of the glass screen next to what appeared to be a control panel. Following the instructions I turned the screen on. I had my choice of a hundred some commercial television channels to choose from, plus sixteen channels that showed different views of the Eagle prior to launch. The container marked "Galley 2" had been moved. I turned off the screen and sat back in my seat. I was still tired, my eyes felt weighted down, and I quickly fell asleep. Once asleep the intense burning feeling returned to my shoulders. I found myself standing inside an apartment burning out of control. The surrounding fire began to crackle and sound louder and then began to roar as the entire building began to shake. I opened my eyes and found that we were beginning to start our journey down the moonrail track. I turned back on the screen and on one channel I saw a side view of us accelerating down the runway. On another channel I could see from a forward angle of our ship moving straight down the track. The passengers sitting near me were as silent as church mice as the five engines ignited with three quarters power. Near the end of the runway the engines came on with full force and pressed us back in our seats. The seats responded to the extra force by becoming pneumatically softer than they were just seconds ago. The shuttle disengaged from the moonrail and up we went into a noticeable climb. I don't know how long I watched, but the land beneath us became smaller and was soon just a short patch of dirt between two immense seas of blue. Who in their right mind would name a planet after such a small exposed portion of the world's surface? The blueberry named Earth soon became small enough to view most of it in my view screen. Real windows were not built in the sides on the shuttle for structural and safety reasons. A quarter inch square pebble traveling through space at unpredictable speeds could crack even the toughest clear polymers.

A heavy "whomp" sound coincided with the activation of an induced gravitational field. It was now safe to get up and get in the way of the working crewmembers. It would be eight hours and two meal services before we reached our destination. I expected to use every single hour to sleep. I am not a cruise ship kind of guy. I never will be. I am all about reaching the destination, not about what pleasures I experience along the way. My journey begins on the moon. The space shuttle is just an expedient method of transportation that I'm required to ride in order to get there.

Page 33

I woke to the sound of the antigrav system powering down and my body feeling suddenly lighter. Retro rockets fired to align us in our final descent towards a thin dark line on the moon's surface. Not much was built on the moon's surface because without an atmosphere, there was nothing to block, stop, or burn up big and small rocks before they hit the moon's surface. It was just safer to avoid all incoming objects and build far beneath the exposed surface. Graded roads led off to various points of interest and ended at underground stations. Event the shuttles went underground before de-boarding the passengers and crew. As we got closer I could see on the video screen moonrail tracks embedded in the middle of each road. A yellow transport bus was clearly visible leaving the main under station called Expom.

Without air to transmit sound, the landing of the Eagle was a quiet non-event. We just felt the touch down and watched on the viewers as we coasted down inside the enclosed terminal area. People wearing yellow space suits directed the Eagle to its final resting dock. A voice came over the intercom and welcomed us to Expom. The seatbelt signs went off and we were able to leave the shuttle. After a short turn around time, the Eagle would be returning to Earth with spent passengers and empty cargo containers. Expom for some would be like a Las Vegas on steroids, but without the luxury of being able to spill water where ever you pleased. And unlike Earth where you could bet your house or your farm, here you could bet an entire country and everyone in it. Expom is the most fabulous cruise ship. Expom is the most spectacular casino. Expom is the greatest tourist and medical center ever envisioned by mankind, and I was here for none of this. I made my way to the reservation desk following a line of so many others.

For the next ten minutes I got the opportunity to rub shoulders with the rich and famous from every nation, who like myself were just another guest when it came to standing around while waiting to check in for a room. It was good to see that no matter how many of their countrymen starved back home, or how many civil wars their countries had survived, or currently were embroiled in there were always a few who rose to the top of economic prosperity in a topsy turvey world and could at least get a chance to unwind and relax on the moon, if not in their own country. Here, it didn't matter where you were from. It didn't matter what religion you were either. Here, Mayans could hypothetically dance with Incans, Protestants could raise a toast with Catholics, and Moslems could tour right along with Jews, Christians, Buddhists, and others. The moon was the perfect place for mankind to become friends with one another; apart from the lack of air, water, and natural resources.

I was at the head of the line when an elderly male representative wearing a rainbow colored vest and a white long sleeve shirt waved me over to the reservation counter. The name on his employee badge read Nigel. With a soft English voice he asked. "May I see your reservations."

I pulled out everything I had which amounted to my passport, a Expom letter head piece of stationary paper with a brief itinerary posted on it, and the stub from my flight ticket.

"Ah, this will do nicely." He picked up my ticket stub and placed it next to a flat qwerty keyboard while he scanned in the information found on my ticket. A flat color television monitor filled with info in the blink of an eye. "Ah Dr. Wilson, we've been expecting you. You have a lovely room on the Sea of Tranquility deck. Take the elevators down two floors and follow the purple arrows." He handed me back my papers, a small guide map, and light chain with a small gold medallion on it like the rectangle ones they sell in Egypt with the picture of a pyramid or some ancient god in the back ground. "Where this around your neck in or on the outside of any clothing, it doesn't matter. It works as an id and a credit card too. Do you have any questions? " I wasn't sure what to ask, but I thought I should think of at least something.

"Uh, my luggage?"

"Naturally, It will be sent to your room shortly. In the mean time make your self at home or gather with other guests for a welcome drink and complimentary appetizers and do have a wonderful time while here." He must have said this same speech a thousand times a day, but there was something about the way he said it that made me feel that he truly meant it.

"Thank you Nigel." I turned and headed for one of the many banks of elevators. I didn't have to wait long and soon found myself in an elevator with a few dignitaries from Kenya, a couple that couldn't take their eyes off each other from Argentina, and two blond haired businessmen who only seemed to enjoy speaking softly in Icelandic.

Upon reaching my floor it was a short walk down the hallway to my room past several pictures that changed images every few seconds and portrayed local sites to visit while at Expom. In front of my room I found myself staring at a glass wall where the door to my room should have been. I found a doorbell on the side of the wall and pressed it. I heard a faint set of chimes from inside the room, but still had no Idea how to get inside.

"Can I help you sir?" I turned to see a thinly built elderly gentleman wearing a purple vest holding a covered tray.

"Ah yes. I'm Dr. Wilson, and this is my room, but I can't seem to enter into my room."

"Oh it must be the biometric sensor sir, I'll have it fixed for you right away." He waved an identification card in front of the door and it slid open.

"If you need anything else sir, name is Kirk, I work security, light maintenance, room service, and anything else you can think of."

"Sounds like you're a busy guy."

"I like to think so sir." I was about to enter the room when a thought occurred to me.

"Mind if I ask you one question, Kirk?"

"Certainly sir?"

"At your age, you could be retired."

"Oh I get that a lot sir. I'm actually a retired mechanical engineer. I came here seven years ago for a heart operation, but the state of my affairs was far worse than the Doctors could have anticipated. They mended me as good as possible, but I'm afraid the return trip as well as Earth's gravity could prove too much for my old ticker."

"So you are stuck here?"

"Quite the contrary sir," he smiled as he replied. "Most people are stuck on Earth and may die prematurely. Here, I may have another twenty years of quality life, good health care, and a chance to meet others such as myself, or even people such as your self. So you can see why I'm always in such a good mood."

"You almost make me want to join you." I said.

"Perhaps when the time is right. Good day sir, and enjoy your stay." With that said he trotted off down the corridor and left me standing in front of the open doorway.

I entered the room and found the room rather large compared to some standard cruise ship cabins. A double wide bed, a sitting chair pushed in to a desk, a few drawers to place clothes, a small curtained off closet, and a small door which led to a compact wash room. Obviously the goal was to keep you busy with activities and out of the room except for sleep. The top of the drawers doubled as a nightstand where a small video screen rested on top. A larger screen hung from a corner wall. I placed my roller bag on top of the desk and began unpacking what few items I was allowed to bring with me. The Transportation Security Administration was getting stricter all the time. You couldn't even bring toothpaste with you unless it was made by *TSA* or one of its subsidiary companies and had the *TSA* proof of purchase sticker boldly visible on the side of the product.

I gave the bed a long hard look. I was tempted to lie down for just a few minutes, but I knew if I did that I would fall into a deep sleep and not wake up until the middle of the night. I had to laugh at that one, because this side of the moon was always daylight. Clocks here were about as useful as they were in northern Canada and Alaska in the summer time. Clocks told you how much longer before you were off work or when a certain television program came on the air via satellite transmission signals, but man made clocks did nothing to help your own internal biological clock adjust according to when the sun was coming up or going down. Until I got back to Earth, if the clock said 11am I would join the throngs of fellow tourists and go eat lunch. If the clock said 11PM I would become a recluse and go to bed. And since it wasn't 11PM yet, it was time to take a quick shower, get rid of the "Ode de Avion" sent I'd acquired while somewhere in flight and go explore the city life at Expom.

I had little trouble finding a bar, there were several on every level. The place was enormously huge compared to my room. A hundred guests, tourists, and inebriated restless souls filled the circular establishment. I didn't recognize the music and it looked too crowded for my tastes, so I turned and headed for the next dotted area on Tranquility level.

The next location had only about fifty people inside listening to music from the late Eighties. The music seemed comfortable like wearing old familiar shoes, so I stepped inside. I looked around for a long narrow bar, a cache of stools, or even an amiable bartender, but all I saw were groups of people huddled around short glass top tables and a small dance floor near the back of the bar. At one of the tables a tubular object raised up near the center of the table. The tube stopped then slid back down into the table leaving a glass filled with ice and some kind of carbonated liquid on top of a small pad. There appeared to be five pads centered in each table like the petals of a daisy flower.

I sat down at a vacant table. My necklace medallion must have activated the computer screen embedded into the tabletop for the minute I sat down, a portion of the table directly in front of me lit up.

Hello DR. Wilson
What would you like to drink?
Then it lit up a picture list of available cocktails, beers, wines, and soft drinks. I touched the screen with my right index finger. The images disappeared. I moved my hand and set it down not far away and a portion of the screen underneath my hand lit up:
Do you wish to converse with another table?
I took my hand off the table so as not to light up any more questions.
Your drink will be right up.
The table screen in front of me lit up. Within a mater of a few seconds the circle facing me in the centered daisy pattern lit up bright blue then lowered into the table itself. I could hear nothing over the other background noise. The blue light emanating from the circular hole suddenly became dimmer and then the blue lit circular pad raised back up into its table height position with a carbonated beverage resting on top. I reached for it and took a sip. It tasted like a typical Bombay gin and tonic, but it came pre-stirred. Looking around the room I could not see one stir stick in sight. The light board on my table came back on and asked me again if I would like to instant message anyone at a nearby table. I

pressed the "**no**" square. It then lit up and asked me if I cared to view the snack screen. Apparently the table screen would keep on asking questions as long as I was willing to participate in any form or to any capacity, so I just ignored the screen and finally the questions ended, the blue circular ring of light deactivated, and I was left to savor my drink in peace. But that moment ended with as little as my second sip when I overheard a conversation in Russian at the next table. I had studied Russian in college and used it for months at a time while working in conjunction with the Russian Fish and Wildlife Service out side of Vladivostok, but that was years ago, and now I wasn't sure how good or accurate my translation abilities still were, but this is what I thought I heard and this is why I tuned in to their conversation and translated it in my head.

"I saw the silver markings too!" a deep feminine Belo Russian voice proclaimed.

"But that was only a small patch. Not like the ones that we saw during the tour." A man's voice countered.

"Well it doesn't matter." A third voice interjected.

"The more important issue is that we all saw something lurking in the shadows and we all agree that we were being watched. So here, the KGB is not dead." The second one said.

"It could have been the Americans," another remarked.

"How ever it was, they gave me the creeps. I was glad to forget about the silver substance and catch up to the rest of the tour," the third one said. They all grunted and drank in agreement.

"I wonder if that was nothing more than an illusion to scare tourists," said a fourth.

"Well, if they were trying to scare ups, the did an excellent job." The female added.

The conversation fell silent as they gulped down their drinks and ordered more.

Russians were the most diluted bunch of paranoid freaks in the world was the only thing I could figure out from over hearing that conversation. It was time to finish my drink and just retire for the night to my room.

Page 42

In the morning I awake to a soft computer synthesized female voice telling me the current time and a swift rundown on my plans for the day. The words of the digitized vocal chords passed through my ears, but I understood or retained little of what she said. I spent half the night tossing and turning in bed. I wasn't really sure where I was until I heard the words "Tranquility Base" then I remembered I was going there today and that in order to do that I had to be physically, if not mentally, on the moon. I wondered if this was what it was like when you began to loose your mind. I got out of bed and took a quick shower and went in search of one of the self-serve cafeterias where you could eat as much as you wanted in spite of the fact that people were still starving to death in selected pervasive locations back on Earth.

I didn't put much on my plate and I ate quickly because I was so excited about the day's events. According to my schedule I was to undertake an expedition moonwalk to the "Sea of Tranquility" and see the site where the first man to walk on the moon had left his footprint. I passed by a brochure stand down the hall and grabbed a few brochures that looked interesting. One of them covered the first American landing site. I glanced at the images and data covering the first step on the moon event. There was the typical image of the glass encased footprints, the adjacent brass dedication placard, the photo taken by the first astronaut of the second man stepping off the ladder of the landing unit, and of course everyone could get their picture taken right next to the same location. I looked at the scheduled departure times and thought If I left now I could make the early bird tour. I wasn't scheduled for the first tour, but there was always someone who slept through the first tour, class, or anything organized for that matter; it was human nature.

Leaving the cafeteria, I quickly found myself standing in the middle of a corridor unfolding maps and trying to find out where I had made a wrong turn. As I stood there like a child lost on the first day of school, a young woman wearing a light blue uniform approached me.

"Do you need any help?" she asked. I recognized the voice then I recognized the face. She was the woman who left the note next to my bed back on Earth. I remember the note because I was so happy to see it, especially after that dream of being trapped in that fire; that was a living nightmare.

"I'm glad to see you, Andrea." I held out my arms and we gave each other a hug. "Any idea where I am? Or what you are doing tonight?" She laughed at my questions,

"To the first of your questions, not to worry, I'll personally take you on a tour of Expom. Now as for the second part, I'm off work at seven. I'll drop by your room if you'd like. If you tried to find me, you would get lost for sure." She smiled and all I could think of doing was staring into her deep hazel eyes. I was hooked, She could have said anything and I would have replied with a resounding "Yes" if I could have made my muscles move any more than a slight nod of my head. She, on the other hand, I had no ideas as to what were her motives, but then again that really didn't seem to be an issue at the moment. Clearly, the moon, my tour, and science in general were nothing compared to the power and might of countless generations of refined reproductive hormones.

"Now let's see," she said as she flipped the pages of her clipboard. "We better get you to Serenity deck so you won't miss your tour." It was amazing how at faster than the speed at which subatomic particles changed phases, the opposite sex could alter your sense of priorities, and then snap you back to reality.

We walked quickly down to Serenity deck and I made it there just in time to hear along with a group of anxious tourists that it would be at least another five minutes before we would start the tour as we were waiting for a few late shows.

"I've got to go," Andrea whispered to me. "See you tonight." Before I could say anything she was gone.

Six minutes later a tall African diplomat of some sort arrived with his entourage and the tour was ready to begin. It's good to be king I thought, even in a mostly socialized world. Then again, I thought, my sister who I hadn't seen in years and had no diplomatic clout what so ever, couldn't make it on time to a blue grass music festival located directly adjacent to her own front porch in her own front yard in her own trailer park. She was perpetually on island time even though she lived in Texas.

"Can I have your attention?" a tall Scandinavian looking gentleman wearing a white Expom uniform said just loud enough to be heard by the entire assembled group. "My name is Steve, and today we are going to take a walk on the moon. We will be going through the doors at the side of the room into the locker room where one of the technicians or myself will help you suit up. After we suit up, we board the moonrail shuttle. Your name will be clearly posted on your helmet and on your assigned locker. Your space suits will look and feel like the original model suits worn by early *NASA* astronauts. The only modification that you will feel is the extra lead weight we added to the boots to keep you from bouncing too high and loosing you balance. After this initial walk, we can remove the extra weight at your discretion. Now if you follow me…" The doors opened and Steve made his way into the locker room. The group quickly followed him inside.

I found my name on a locker, as did the rest of the tour group. I waved my hand in front of my name as I saw the group leader do in front of another locker and my locker door opened and then recessed into the wall and out sight. Before me were all the parts that came together to make an air tight, thermo insulated, Mark 5 moon suit. The Mark 5 suit was state of the art, but looked in all respects like the first space suits ever worn on the moon to give the individual tourist a sense of nostalgia and give the tours a historical perspective that modern form fitting pressure suits couldn't visually pull off.

I glanced to my right and watched as two Expom attendants helped a female tourist put on the Mark 5 pants and then connect her boots. I followed suit, but managed to do it all on my own. I noticed that the boots were weighted with extra lead. I guess that's how they keep us tourists from dancing around like wild bunnies every time we took a step in the reduced gravity on the moons actual surface. Someone from Expom had requested my measurements prior to my leaving Earth and from what I could tell so far; the suit and boots matched my size perfectly.

I was just in the middle of putting on the top piece when an attendant came over and lent me some assistance. He helped me place the top over my arms and chest and snapped it in place against my torso.

"I bet you're a diver?" he said as he helped me put one of my gloves on.

"Yeah, drysuits." I said as the glove snapped in place.

"I thought so. I'll let you put the over glove on while I find someone who really needs some assistance. "Don't put the helmet on yet. We do that one at a time near the shuttle boarding door."

"Thank you," I said as he stepped away. I put on the other glove and snapped it in place. I looked around and helped an elderly man a meter away from me snap on his boots and then helped him with the top piece. One of the assistants gave me a thumb up signal.

Once everyone on the tour was suited up. We carried our helmets over to the shuttle platform access door. Square white colored air recycle packs were suspended waist high on a conveyor belt storage rack system. I, along with everyone else, watched as one of the tour guides dressed as we were, sat on a bench directly in front of the rack with his back facing a protruding air pack. The assembly line sensors responded to sensors on the back of his suit and within seconds an air pack attached itself to his back. He then stood and moved to the side.

"Putting on your air tanks is that easy." He said to the group. "There are four different bench stations in this room, so help your self when you are ready." He pointed in various directions with his gloved hand.

The Guide helped a tourist sit down, and before the tourist had a chance to bring his arms down to his sides, an air pack was firmly attached to the back of his moon suit. The guide then led the tourist out of the way over to the shuttle entrance door to wait for all the tourists to follow both of their leads and don their own air packs. At the entrance door to the shuttle when all the tourists had donned their air packs, which was a surprisingly quick process, the lead guide placed his helmet on in slow motion for all those in attendance to see. He held it up high, lowered it over his head, and when it was sealed just right, a thin green circular strip of light lit up for a brief moment around the connection joint of each boot, glove, waist, and neck area. His space suit unit was sealed and good to go. He waved to everyone then proceeded through the shuttle entrance door. Each tourist in turn with the aid of Expom attendants set their helmet in place over their heads, verified that all lights were green, then entered the shuttle moonrail car. From what I could tell, everyone's joints sealed perfectly and the process flawlessly took mere minutes. No matter what culture you were from or language you spoke, the assembly line process was easy to follow. These people really knew what they were doing.

With my helmet on and secure I felt a rush of fresh cooling sensation enwrap my body. I stepped aboard the shuttle and took a vacant seat. For all newcomers to Expom, the first tour was always to the site of the first manned landing on the moon. The area itself had been roped off so people could only look at the remains on the first footprints on the moon and walk around the periphery of the site. Keeping it preserved helped people to imagine what it must have been like for the first men to walk on the moon with the thought that what they were doing was more than unique, but the greatest exploratory journey ever achieved by mankind.

The moonrail shuttle cars moved along the track and on the way the guide gave a historical narrative of the moon and I'm not sure what else as I was not really listening. Tourists asked him questions and he gave elaborate responses, but all I saw was the bleak landscape pocked with craters of every size and variety out the surrounding windows. The surfaces looked like what you would find under a heavily used charcoal grill plate. I was on a tour to hades, but the broilers had broken down that day. I wondered if this is what we as a race expected to find here or if as a higher intellect species we would go anywhere just to transmit back home a signal or post card.

I'm on the near side of the moon today. We're off to explore the far side of the moon tomorrow. If it's not too dark, I'll send a note from there too. Hope all is well. Sincerely

Buck and Addie Venturous

The total time on board the moonrail shuttle was under and hour and soon we were approaching the sacred site.

"As you disembark the moonrail, watch your step as this will be the first time many of you have ever felt the full effects of light gravity." I have no idea who said it, the voice just came over the speaker in my head set. From what I understood, the guides could listen to us and talk to us from anywhere at anytime, but tourists could only talk to one another if we were less than six maters apart. I figured that was so we could fan out and communicate privately with whom we so desired.

I was one of the last to get off the shuttle. I had a good view of others trying to catch their balance on the moon's surface. It was weird watching them stumble, but with no air to transmit the sounds our boots made scraping against the rocks the sight looked surreal. I heard the voices of two tour guides in my helmet trying to help the tourists acclimate to the lighter than Earth's gravity feeling. Just like others who heeded the advice of the tour guides, I quickly found that a light bunny hop was a good way to make forward motion progress. I bunny hopped a little harder until I found myself flat on my back looking up at some stars, that for the life of me I couldn't recognize.

"Up you go," a guide said to me as she helped me to my feet. Before I could say thank you, she hopped away to help the next tourist inexplicably looking up at the stars. Welcome to the Sea of Humiliation, I thought to myself.

I quickly became accustomed to the difference in gravity, for as a scuba diver I had years of experience with feeling weightless. It was just the first few steps that always proved so tricky; too over anxious, too cocky, and too sure of one's self.

As I hopped, then skipped around, I saw the blue marble named Earth positioned between the stars and thought about how it must have felt for the early astronauts to be looking at their mother planet and somewhere in the back of their minds wondering if they would make it back to their loved ones. At that point in time, they were the only ones in space. At least when you drive through the deserts to Las Vegas you have emergency phones placed every 60-100 of miles. Help was just hours away; not days away...if at all. Early astronauts were true gamblers. They didn't need Reno silver dollars, Vegas chips, just their lives. They won the chance to explore another world and set us farther apart from apes. If I had had a leg bone with me, I would have thrown it up towards the stars with unbridled passion and pride.

PAGE 52

By the time we boarded the moonrail shuttle to make our way back to Expom, most of us had acclimated to the moon's gravity. We spent over an hour jumping, hopping, and skipping around a site of encased footprints and a flag of the United States. Like any good tourist, our current quest to explore and conquest space had been satiated and now it was time to discover what was back at the ranch for lunch.

The trip back seemed fast, but not fast enough. I had to listen to everyone talking about his or her personal experience at the site. We were all there, we all saw it, and all logged it in our memory, but that didn't seem to matter. Everyone took turns interrupting each other to tell their side of the experience. I looked at my air gauge as we rode back home. I still had over 14 hours of air left according to my gauge; talk about a built in safety factor.

The rest of the day tour members were free to enjoy the facilities of Expom, or for those who were still suffering from jet lag, it was time for a quick nap before attending the evening's events.

After I returned my moon suit to my locker, I proceeded to the handball courts to squeeze in a couple of games. The handball courts were located in the left wing of Expom, which because of the distance, seemed to be an exercise in itself just trying to get there. When I reached the handball courts I found out why they were so remotely situated. I stood in the balcony and watched as a couple of players new to the sport try their best to play the game. The courts were the same as those on Earth, except that the ceiling was padded. But the ball was different and so was the gravity. The padded ceiling seemed to be a godsend for the current two players as they continually cushioned their heads against it. They would start running after the ball and without the power of Earth's gravity to keep them off the walls, they just ran up the sides in pursuit of the ball. If they had been using the same hardball as used on Earth, they might have killed themselves. The ball they used looked softer and was neon yellow with crisscrossing thick black stripes. The size of the ball looked the same, but as I watched the couple play, I could see that the ball did not hit the intended surfaces as hard. The ball cushioned inward before the full force on the hand made contact. Yet even with this reaction the ball returned to the far wall with a force equal to what I was accustomed to witnessing on Earth. One of the more interesting aspects to playing under these conditions was the basic sense of adventure.

Having seen enough, I decided to go down and give the game a try for myself. I found a vacant court and proceeded to cautiously hit the ball. I felt a little tipsy and had to replant my feet on several occasions to maintain balance. I also notice that although the air eventually slowed the ball down the ball lowered its height only in painstakingly in small increments. It was much like watching a bullet ricochet off the walls but without the eventual rate of decent my brain took for granite. I soon learned that hitting the ball and keeping it up in the air was a breeze. The trick to this moon ball game was all about the landing, not hitting your head on the ceiling, and most importantly not hitting you face on the floor. With a few abrasions on my head and face, I felt I was ready to find an opponent.

I found a tall muscular black man practicing by himself a few courts rooms away. He had good coordination in the gravity-reduced environment. I knew I didn't stand a chance against him, but I asked to play against him just the same.

"Mind playing a game with me?" I asked. "I'm a beginner." He looked at me as if I was a long lost family member and came over to me to shake my hand.

"I'm Jason. I'd be honored." I thought that this was a little too formal for a practice game with a stranger, but this was Expom, and customs could be anything you wanted on the moon. He looked like he wanted to say something else, but then seemed to think better of it, so I took my set position and we started to play

While I would walk towards the ball, he would jump and save precious time in reaching the on coming ball. I tried to copy every move he made and by the end of our second round I actually scored a few points. In an impromptu break he shook my hand again.

"Nice work." he said. "You catch on fast." I was really beginning to like this game and he was a great athlete. We played two more rounds before I was spent. During that time I found out that Jason was employed at Expom although he didn't say where. He played a lot when off duty and said I could join him any time. When I left, he was still playing against himself and for all I knew, he looked like he was winning.

After the great experience at moon ball I marched triumphantly back to my room, took a shower, and got ready to go out for the night. It wasn't until I was putting on my pants that an electronic note popped up on my television screen from Andrea stating she was working over in reservations ant that If I wanted to, I could stop by around seven and visit for an hour. I didn't write back, but I would be there with pants all the way on.

I had no problem tracing my steps back to the reservations area. I ended up arriving a little early so I took a seat and watched all the strange and exotic people pass by.

"Mind if I join you?" A tall light skinned dark haired woman asked. The woman sat down before I had a chance to respond. "My name is Cynthia. You must have just recently arrived, because I'm sure I would have remembered meeting you before." Her voice sounded very seductive. A light sent of hibiscus permeated the air around her. Her naturally tanned skin was void of any imperfections. Her blue –gray eyes were mesmerizing, but her approach felt wearily calculated.

"I," was all I got out before I was interrupted.

"John, sorry I kept you waiting," Andrea said as she approached us. She had a big smile planted on her face. She gave not the slightest indication of Cynthia's presence.

"Well, if you will excuse me," Cynthia said to no one in particular. She unseated herself and left almost as quickly as she had arrived.

"Well, I see you haven't had any difficulty meeting anyone." Andrea grinned.

"Not really," I smiled and replied.

"Don't look too smug. She works here . . . Unofficially of course."

"I should have known," I said. "A woman out of the blue comes over to strike up a conversation? Not very likely back on Earth either."

"Do you like sushi?" she asked. She must have already known what my answer would be.

"We had a fresh shipment of seafood dock about two hours ago. You can't get any fresher than that on this side of the moon." I stood up and she entwined her left arm in my right arm and escorted me down one of the halls.

As we sat down at a busy counter in front of a Japanese Chef obsessed with how precisely even he sliced every fish and how perfectly he placed a slice of meat on each piece on a small pre-formed block of rice, we had a chance to chat a little.

"I have to admit that I'm a little confused," I began.

"About the note I left you? I'm known for having a thing for scientists."

"I see, but that doesn't exactly explain the note."

"Don't worry Dr. Wilson it all will in due time. Are you enjoying you stay here?" I nodded yes, and with that our meticulously prepared meal arrived. We ate in almost total silence, as the tiny morsels were too good and flavorful to let linger on our plates. Unfortunately, when finished with our meal, it was time for her to go back to work.

"Thanks for joining me on such short notice," Andrea said as we were about to part.

"Anytime," I replied and I meant it.

"Good, I'll be in touch." I waved at her as she went through a door marked employees only.

Not really knowing what to do next I decide to try my luck at gambling at one of the many nearby casino halls. When I went inside the mermaid motif casino I recognized two of the men that were on my tour earlier in the day. They were the same two that I unfortunately had to over hear their entire life stories during the moonrail shuttle ride. The short plump one was named Dean and he sported a minimum amount of gray hair on his head in the shape of elongated sideburns. The other gentleman, Garret, was tall and thin and sported a short crew cut with a full crop of blonde hair. The two of them were thick as thieves in conversation and so I tried to reverse my steps and get out of the casino before they spotted me, but it was already too late.

"Hey John," Garret shouted above the music other voices and the sounds of the poker machines. "Come over here and join us."

I noted the slurred voice, but I didn't hesitate to step over to them, as I had the feeling that Garret would call out to me again and even speak up louder next time.

"Hi guys, I see you're having a good time." Both of them had glassy eyes, and holding glasses filled with green swirling strands around what appeared to be a scotch based substance.

"It's number 49 A on the machine." Dean slurred. "You gotta try it." Garret was already ordering another round on the console.

"Sure, I'll give it a try. Did you guys enjoy the tour today?" I asked.

"It was alright," Garret said as he handed me a drink. "Funny thing happened though."

"What was that?" I asked just trying to keep the conversation going.

"Well, Dean and I came back to the shuttle before the rest of the group, so we decided to take a quick walk around the moonrail tracks. Any way, we came across this large boulder on not far away so we decided to take a look at it. Dean and I had had a couple of drinks before the tour started, so I guess because of that we were a little careless. The next thing we know we had this oily silver stuff all over our pants and boots. I absent-mindedly took a sip of the strange concoction, which I found tasted minty, but not too sweet.

"I'm sorry, what did you say?" I asked.

"Not so loud." Garret continued. "We cleaned it off. All of it. It took a little effort though. I think we got it on us when we tried to climb the bolder."

"Did anyone see you guys?"

"Just one of the guides. He helped us brush the stuff off of our suits."

"Do you remember his name?"

"I think his name was Clifford," Dean said. "But why do you want to know that?"

"I may want to talk to him. Last night I overheard a group talking about a similar material. They also thought that they were being watched."

"So what?" Garret asked. He looked intensely into his glass of swirling green elixir. "We had the stuff on us and we didn't feel like we were being watched. I think the guy just thought he saw something. Probably watches too many horror movies".

"That's something I'd like to find out for myself," I said.

"When?" Dean asked.

"Tomorrow sounds good," I said as I raised my glass. I left it vague as possible. Garret raised his glass high in the air and said, "Here's to the moon monster. May he keep the shiny stuff off of us." Dean and Garret drank to the toast while I smiled and shook my head. They were definitely a crazy pair, I thought. A group of very attractive women entered the casino and at that point the matter at hand was forgotten.

Page 63

After a few more rounds of 49-A, more than just the slot machine wheels were spinning out of control. Dean and Garret became my best long lost buddies, and frankly, we were all higher than Earth's outer orbit.

As I made my way back to my room I stopped by the reservation counter to try and catch a glimpse of Andrea, but she was nowhere in sight. Which was fortunate, considering the less than intellectual appearance I was in, so I softly began singing to myself and continued on my way.

"It's me John," I growled at the door to my room. I gave the sensor a menacing glare. A second later the door slid open. I swaggered into the room. "Thank you very much," I begrudgingly added. I wanted to say more to the door, but it was then that I heard noise coming from the direction of my bathroom that stopped me in my tracks. I heard the shower running and someone was definitely not conserving my hotel guest allocation share of recycled water. Before I could take another step the shower stall door opened and a wet arm and torso region of what was definitely female in nature reached out and snatched a towel off a hook. I stood staring as the female got out of the shower with her back to me and wrapped the towel around her hair. She then took a second towel and wrapped it around her body.

"I thought we were supposed to conserve resources," I said. She whirled around to face me.

"Oh, you scared me. You're right about the towels though, which one would you have me put back?" She looked at me with a big devious smile on her face."

"Well, I'd hate to see your wet hair get cold."

"You're ever the gentleman." She walked past me and sat near the head of the bed.

"I try. Would you like something to drink?"

She reached in her purse and pulled out a silver packet of what appeared to be throat lozenges.

"No thanks. Would you care for a couple of Merrils?" I had heard of Merrils, but never had seen them in the wrapper. They were Marijuana tablets laced with a psilocybin derivative.

"They're a great sex stimulator." She added.

"I'll pass. Seeing you in nothing but towels, seems to be working just fine."

"Do you mind if I do?" she asked.

"Not at all." Right about now she could have put vanilla pudding in her hair and I would have cared less. She seemed to sense what I was thinking. She took the Merrils and swallowed them dry then reached up to feel underneath the towel.

"Oh, my hair's still wet."

"It's dry enough for what I have in mind," I said.

"Oh wow," she said.

"What's the matter?"

"I didn't expect them to kick in so fast." She lay back down with towels and all on the pillow. She looked relaxed with a big smile on her face. She closed her eyes. The room in her opinion was turning soft and fuzzy. I walked over to her and picked up the packet of Merrils. I read the label and began to laugh. She opened her eyes.

"What's so funny?"

"Nothing really," I said. "Promise me you won't do anything too strenuous like operate heavy machinery for the next couple of hours?" I gave her the most serious look I could muster. She rolled her eyes, then rolled her body over and touched a black panel square on the wall with her right hand. A small section of glass paneling lit up.

"What would you like to hear?" she asked with a sudden soft sensual tone to her voice. I was too busily examining every exposed posed portion of her body to care what we were listening to.

"I think you'll like this." Her fingers danced over the glass surface. "Are you going to just stand there or are you going to join me in bed?" I pulled my shirt over my head as quickly as I could without regard for buttons or possible stretch and tears. By the time my shirt past up and over my head the room had darkened and the walls were alive with a 360 degree view of some spectacular tropical sandy beach. I heard the waves breaking on the sand and smelt a slight citrus scent in the air. If she wanted to make love on the beach, that was just fine by me, but then again, so was anywhere else.

PAGE 72

The next morning Andrea woke to a very familiar sound. It was the automatic reminder signal that my tour was about to begin within an hour. She jumped out of my bed and hurriedly collected her belongings.

"I've got to run," She said as she threw on her clothes. I just lay in bed and admired the fast paced show. She gave me a smirk and then kissed me quickly on the lips and said, "See you tonight." She paused for one last look in the mirror and then left my quarters as if escaping the scene of a fire.

"Bye," I said to the door and myself. I took a brief minute to shave and shower and out the door I went too.

This time I knew right where I was going and it didn't take me long to reach the locker room. Today I was scheduled to tour a site not far from Expom. We were going to explore the famous moon cave and we would be back in time for the Mexican buffet on level three. Since this side of the moon always had the same amount sunlight. The term "Afternoon" had little proximal relevance.

Expom was built in a crater impact zone close to a cavern in order to reduce construction costs as well as to be close to one particular tourist attraction. An endless maze of tunnels ran in all directions beneath and/or around Expom. Some of them were nothing more than natural pockets in the moons subsurface crust connected by naturally made tunnels, while others were man made. Most passages were well marked, but a few were a bit confusing even for some of the locals. That's why it was mandatory that master guides escort tourists and tourists could only enter those areas that had been roped off and were specially designated areas. At least that's what I remember reading in one of the info guides.

I entered the locker room and spotted Dean next to his locker. I could only assume that Garret was nearby.

"Hi John." Dean shouted out. I smiled and walked towards him. I raised my hand and greeted him not knowing what else to do.

"How are you feeling to today Dean?" I lost count on the number of drinks he had put away last night. It was far more than I could even put away in my youth, and that didn't bring back pleasant memories.

"I've been better." He turned his jogging shirt inside out and back again. I wasn't sure the purpose of this activity. He saw me grinning.

" I don't see the lipstick on your cheek, but you've definitely been enjoying your stay here more than us." Dean said. I wasn't sure how he knew; perhaps it was just the nature of my grin that gave it away. "I mean it's bad enough that you didn't share with us, but do you have to rub it in as well?" I wondered just what kind of subliminal facial cues he had been able to read. Was I that obvious?

"Sorry, I'll try a more dead pan expression next time I great you."

"That's not exactly the solution I had in mind," Dean laughed.

At that moment I heard heavy footsteps and turned to see someone in a moon suit with a helmet on and sun visor down coming right up to me.

"Hi Garret," I said. The visor whipped up and there was the sad expression on Garret's face.

"Oh man, how did you know?"

"Garret, I only know two people on the moon, and Dean is already standing next to me."

"That's not true," Dean piped in. He knows a female and he's been cheating on us."

Garret gave me an evil eye. "You bastard, don't you know that as musketeers we share and share alike?"

"No one told me."

"We'll let him off this time Garret." They both looked strangely at me. " But in the future, either share the treasures, or face the measures."

I wasn't quite sure what to say, my newfound friends seemed to be slightly off their rockers.

I started putting on my moon suit in preparation for the tour. As soon as the entire group was suited up one of the tour guides directed us aboard the shuttle bus. I headed for the tail bus to avoid the crowd, but Garret grabbed me by the arm and stopped me in my tracks.

"Wait a minute. We have something to show you." I glimpsed Dean trying to suppress his own laughter. I was weary of all this attention, but my curiosity got the better of me so I followed Garret and Dean inside the packed forward compartment. The two sat down on a bench directly across from a Russian official of some sort. I recognized his face from the Internet. The man was sitting next to a younger woman and another man that appeared to be his bodyguard, but with moon suits on, it was hard to tell for sure. However the waistline on the recognizable Russian's moon suit looked distended as did the shoulder and arm joints on the bodyguard's suit. The three of them were eying all the other occupants of the shuttles as if the cold, the KGB, and food lines were still in practice. Since the days of Ivan the terrible, the psychological scares on Russian people never seemed to rest in peace. Germans rebuilt fruitful lives and over came the memories of Hitler, but Russians feared that another bad seed like Stalin or worse could come along with the next crop of wheat or generation of citizens, so layers of psychological security and a guarded existence meant long term economical and political survival. Perhaps that was why Russia still struggled to this very day, while its former communist ally China, without this deeply rooted psyche, had become an economical super powerhouse. Then again, perhaps it all boiled down to luck, and no country was as old, as big, or as lucky as China.

As my mind drifted back to where I currently was, I could see that Dean and Garret were laughing to themselves for no apparent reason. It seemed odd, but so were they.

"You want to tell me what's so funny?" I regretted asking the moment the words were out of my mouth.

"Turn your personal radio transmitter off." Dean said. The personal transmitter only transmitted 3 meters or so. So one didn't have to listen to the entire group of tourist yakking away. The group radio was received and broadcast by all, but you could turn off the other tourists and listen only to the guides if you preferred. I had no clue what the emergency buttons did. I complied and Dean reached over and cupped his hands against my helmet. You see the Russian sitting over there?" I nodded back at Dean. "We slipped a piece of cheese into the man's boot, just before he suited up." Dean could hardly keep a straight face as he spoke to me." Once again I didn't know what to say, so I just sat back in my chair. These two clowns were planning childish pranks well in advance, and I would go to great lengths to ensure I never got on their bad side, but how to get away from them without causing precisely my dreaded fear to be the unalterable outcome?

The three of us didn't speak another word until we arrived at our destination. Dean and Garret looked at the Russians from time to time and the Russians kept an obvious eye on the three of us. The random chuckles of Dean and Garret did not diffuse the situation in anyway.

When the shuttle stopped, the Russians left the compartment as fast as they could. Dean and Garret started to laugh uncontrollable as soon as the Russians were out of site. I turn back on the close up radio signal, and so did the two pranksters.

"Did you really put something in his boot?" They both stopped chuckling and looked at me as if I hadn't heard a word they said.

"Limburger," Garret said matter of fact. "It's wrapped in a piece of flat plastic so that the more he walks the better things should get."

"So you specifically targeted him?" They both just shook their heads. Dean finally spoke up. We got the idea before we got here. With the body guard and all, he just looked like a good candidate."

I wondered what they might have in store for me? Especially now that I knew that it wasn't the person they targeted, just the opportunity.

Outside the bus we were told what was expected of us and once again they told us what we could not do, which seemed to be everything except following close behind the tour guides. We formed a couple of small groups. We were standing on a raised platform a meter above the real moon's surface as if they were purposely keeping us from stepping foot on the moon. We were close to the base of a huge wall of impacted surface crust. The wall stood almost 60 meters straight up. The spectacle had been one of many oddities formed by the smashing and crushing effects of countless meteors and even though the bulk of the moon had been formed by the an iron laden meteor smashing into the Earth a few billion years ago and ejected fragments from that explosion, some from Earth's crust and some from the meteor's crust, formed the spherical shape of the moon, impacts and changes on the moon's surface kept occurring. Most small objects entering the Earth's atmosphere at his speed burnt up, but the moon, with no atmosphere had no such natural defenses.

Near the center of the wall near the base ran a crack that was wide enough for an entire group of tourists to walk through at one time. I had read about the labyrinth of caves and tunnels that awaited us inside the entrance. In front of the cave one of the tour guides turned and spoke through the radios in our helmets. "Ok people, turn you helmet lights on." Actually, I think the guides had been talking all along, but I wasn't really listening to them until now.

I turned on my helmet light, but hung back towards the end of the tour procession. Dean and Garret went ahead of me. I didn't want their distraction while I took in the sights and day dreamed about life on other planets.

The first thing I noticed when stepping through the opening were long corridors of rope and placards attached to the walls at waist high level. There was no way you could get lost or accidentally get off the right trail. I marched quietly behind a group of people thrilled at seeing the underside of gray rock.

The trail winded up and down and finally leveled off as we entered into a large underground cavern. A little larger and it would have made a fine indoor soccer arena. There were traces of minerals here from meteors and it gave the room the appearance of a giant piece of painted artwork. At first glace it looked spectacular, then a second later I was over it. The rocks began to remind me of dead coral reefs, but even dead coral reefs had passing fish and something to look at. Ok, so I was already over the whole moon experience and wanted to go diving somewhere tropical like Bonaire, or Grand Caymans.

The rest of the tour was much more of the same. I actually found myself catching up to Dean and Garret just to make the time spent on the tour more interesting. Near the end of the excursion the tunnels became small and the scenery was back to a simple yet unassuming gray motif. We had walked, skipped, and jumped for over forty minutes and some of the tourists were still back with the guides in the main cavern while other tourists were just falling behind. The tour guide leading the forward section was new and not too prepared to deal with over active tourists. Dean, Garret, and I got a little ahead of him and before he new it; we were out of his sight. Once far enough away, Garret stopped by a roped off tunnel section and lifted up the rope. Dean ducked and marched right under it and I did too for fear of being a spoiled sport. It was pure mischievous adventure with no objective in mind and no regard for our safety. We were three boys swinging out over the Mississippi River with no clue that bull sharks sometimes entered these fresh waters.

We went down what seemed to be a distantly used trail. Dean led the way as he was first to duck under the rope. I was in second place and Garret was last only because he led the rope for us to go under. Our lights scanned the walls for side branch trails, but we found no others to get lost in. 30 meters into our journey the trail bent around the corner. We were forced to stop and would have to turn back. How boring was that. We could hear the rest of the group as they neared the point of our diversion. Garret stepped past us and faced the wall of stone. I saw him hold up a rock and place it against the wall. He started to scratch the letter G into the wall. Given time, he probably would have written his whole name and the date he first stepped foot on the moon, but it was never meant to be. The ground that we were standing on began to shake. Dean and I stepped back from the bend and the ground seemed to be more stable here, But Garret was so intent on his graffiti mission that he stayed put. That is until the ground gave out below him and he felt himself slowly falling through the floor of the cave.

"Huh? Whoa," he yelled out. The tremor stopped. Dean and I looked quickly at each other then back around the corner where we last saw Garret," but he was not there. There was part of the letter G and a line moving down the wall, and a hole in the walkway with a faint light coming from beneath the substrate. Garret landed with out cracking his helmet or hearting himself.

"Hey Guys, you still up there?" We could hear him, but we didn't see him. Dean looked over the edge of the hole. He fell flat down on his chest and lowered his arms before I knew what he was doing.

"Grab my boots, John. Garret, take my hand." I did as instructed and apparently Garret did too, for I saw him being helped up out of the hole and over to what appeared to be a safe spot.

"Well, that was Exciting," Garret spoke up as he caught his breath.

"What was down there?" Dean asked.

"Just more tunnels. The place must be more riddled than Rome."

"Are you alright?" I asked.

"I broke my pride, but nothing that can't be fixed." Garret began brushing himself off. I saw specks of a silver substance rub off is pants and disappear with the dust on the ground. I turned and headed back towards the main tunnel. Garret was right behind me. Dean must have stopped to look down the hole because it took him a minute to reach us back at the main trailhead. This time I held the rope up for Garret and a minute later for Dean to pass under.

"Did you see that silver stuff?" Dean asked as he passed under the rope.

" I did, but now's not the time." I said. " Let's catch up with the rest of the tour."

"I'll second that," Garret said as he stretched his back. Perhaps he was a little sorer than he first let on.

PAGE 84

As we caught up to the rest of the tour group I could see the expression of the tour guide's face who was responsible for our group change from a look of panic to one of utter relief as he know could confirm his count and his job was no longer on the line.

We were all in one way or another still shaken up by our experience, but when we saw the expression on the unfortunate Russian our moods changed dramatically. We quickly forgot about our ordeal and instead thought about Limburger cheese being mashed by his foot. The Russian's face displayed a very bleak expression. He was pale and looked like he was going to pass out. My guess is that he had been in this condition soon after he stepped off the shuttle. What a mean trick I thought to myself. I wondered what they might have in store for me? Like the old book on the Art of War said, keep your friends close, but keep your enemies closer.

Somehow the tour finished not far from the entrance to the cave. Some tourists hopped, others skipped, and others seemed to crawl back to the entrance of the cave. I was puzzled at first, but after retracing the trail in my head, it seemed to work out. I stepped on board the shuttle bus right behind Dean and Garret.

We sat away from the Russians on this leg of our journey, but from my vantage point I could see that the man was suffering badly. His bodyguard appeared perplexed and had no idea how to help his ill stricken boss. The female companion refused to look in his direction in case whatever he had might inflict her too. Needless to say, Dean and Garret were extremely proud of their deed and were still snickering from time to time during the journey back to Expom.

The minute the shuttle stopped, the Russian found a burst of energy. He jumped to his feet, pushed by everyone else, and was one of the first to disembark the shuttle. His actions were so quick and precise that his bodyguard was caught unprepared and only as an after thought scurried after his master like a wayward dog. The Russian official passed through the airlock and into the locker room at Olympic speed. He quickly removed his helmet and gasped for fresh air. His bodyguard burst through the door just in time to receive an evil glare. The guard nervously tried to swallow, but couldn't get over the lump in his throat.

"Help me take this suit off." Although there was a rancid odor permeating around the Russian, his bodyguard dutifully stepped forward and helped as much as he could. The foul odor quickly spread around the locker room.

The rest of the tour group came through the doors just in time to acquire a full dose of the obnoxious odor. Several people turned pale and one of the tour guides adjusted the air conditioning system on a far wall. The room soon became tolerable and the tourists began changing out of their suits as quickly as possible.

The Russian changed into his street clothes and combed through his assigned suit for any evidence of tampering. A small slip of yellow tainted cellophane wrapping fell out of his boot. What was ever inside the wrapping was gone now. He put the wrapper in his pocket. He would have it tested when he got back home.

From the other end of the room I peeked now and then to see if the Russian had found the cause of his turmoil. I saw him hold up a piece of cellophane to the light and then disappointedly put it in his pocket. I was puzzled just as much as the Russian as I saw nothing of substance in the bag. Limburger cheese could be smashed and mashed, but didn't disintegrate without a trace. I looked away before the Russian caught me staring, but only by a fraction of a second.

"Man did I get my suit dirty." Garret said as he looked down at his pile of gear.

"Try a different bar tonight?" Dean asked. He could have cared less about the current condition of Garret's suit.

"What was that silver stuff you had on your pants?" I asked Garret.

"Beats me, but it wiped off."

"You call yourself a chemical engineer?" Dean butted it.

"Look, I've never seen anything like it before." Garret replied.

"I'm sure they can tell us a the Science Center." I said.

"Great John, you go there. Garret and I will meet you back at the bar. We're only interested in colored liquids and silver laden babes."

I had the feeling that I was being set up for something. I set my gear inside my locker and pressed my finger on the electronic code to lock it. I said good-bye and headed down out of the room. One of the guides eyed me as I left the room.

Page 90

The science center was relatively easy to find. Either that, or I was getting use to finding my way around Expom. Just like those cruise ships appeared to be overwhelming at first glance, but by the second day on a cruise ship I could almost tell you the exact number of steps it took to get from the main pool to the hamburger bar. Anyway, during certain hours of the day, which I forgot, the science center would be open with someone on duty to answer any questions any of the tourists may have about the moon or the other orbiting planets in our solar system. At least I remembered reading this much in a brochure.

Looking through the glass door I could see that the room looked smaller than the image of the science center in the brochure. There were a few couches with a few books on the shelves, but what I was after was a chat with the man who was hunched over in his chair. I had no idea what he was doing, but what ever it was, it currently took all of his concentration.

A sensor activated as I stepped inside the room. The man at the desk raised his head and with a quick few key strokes shut down his main screen and pulled the papers laid out in front of him into one disorganized pile. He looked anemic. He had black hair and long sideburns. His eyes were dark brown and lifeless and he was void of any facial expressions. As far as ethnic background went, he could have been part Caucasian and Asian, European and Native American Indian, or any other mixture for that mater. It was as if he could have blended in with almost any community and no one would have paid him much attention.

"And what can I do for you?" he quietly whispered. It was as if it pained him to get the few words out. I could barely hear him, so I made my way towards him before I answered him.

"Sure, who are you?" I asked. The man looked perplexed.

"I'm Doctor Slatski. Head of the moon geological survey team." I heard of the them before, but they lost all of their limelight after the survey team on Venus ventured forth. I held out my hand.

"I'm Dr. Wilson. I would like some information on a substance that my friends and I encountered on our tour."

"Oh, so you're a geologist?"

"No," I said. "Marine Biologist."

"Oh, that's probably just one of the effects of our lighting system. It reflects in shimmer waves off the dirt."

"No this wasn't soil, it was something else."

"I'm not sure I understand you," he said.

"We encountered the material at an undisclosed location while on our tour earlier today."

"An undisclosed location, on a tour?

"Sort of. The substance was bright silver, even in reduced light."

"Sounds interesting, but I would have to see a sample before I could give you an educated guess."

I heard what he said, but I didn't reply. My only sample had been wiped away by Dean and Garret. For the first time, I had the feeling that it might have all been a hoax or a prank, and I may have been the intended victim.

"Sorry to bother you." I said. I turned to leave, but then had one last thought. "By the way, have you explored the tunnels below the tour trails?" I could see the surprise in his eyes, but he quickly recovered.

"There are no trails, just cracks and fissures where you could get injured. Stay on the trails Dr. Wilson."

"Thank you Dr. Slatski." I turned and left this time. I had the distinct impression he was trying to hide something. He could have also been part of Dean and Garrets practical joke. I was beginning to feel a little paranoid. It was too early to go to a bar, so I decided to try and forget about everything and go play tourist.

I left the center and went to the pub where I thought my new buddies might be hanging out. Both of them were standing next to the bar. A woman dressed in little more than green glitter was dancing on top of the bar right in front of them. She was tall and slender and seemed to have the right proportions for whatever alien race she was attempting to sexily portray. As I moved closer I could see a thin dark green streak running down from the left side of her forehead and terminating precariously below her belly button.

I tapped Garret on the shoulder. Dean saw Garret turn and he in turn looked my way. He said something, but I couldn't hear anything but the heavy base music. I pointed over to an empty booth and was surprised when they actually moved from the spot light and the glitter of the girl on stage.

"I suppose you want to talk about that silver stuff again." I cocked my head and looked at Garret. I couldn't tell if he was toying with me with some elaborate gag or he was showing real interest. I went for the bait.

"As a matter of fact I do. Did either of you notice anything unusual while we were returning to the main trail?"

"Yeah, I hurt more than my pride when I fell down that tunnel."

"No, not that."

"You mean like that silver stuff I picked up and put in my pocket? Dean asked.

"You mean you have a piece?" I dubiously inquired.

"Well I did, but when we got back here, it was gone."

"Of course it was. Are you two pulling my leg?"

"No, it really was gone. Maybe it dissolved or something."

"Sure, Garret," added. "Maybe it evaporated like all the other gas you've been lett'n off lately." I still couldn't figure out if I was being played or not. Dean shrugged his shoulders

"Well, do either of you remember seeing it when we first entered the tunnel?" Both of them shook their heads no. I don't think any of us saw it, because it wasn't there when we first entered the tunnel," I pointed out.

"You think someone put it there to scare us?" Dean quickly glanced around the room as if expecting to catch someone eaves dropping on his very words, or some mysterious creature to run up and pounce on him, wasn't sure which way his brain really would go, but those were the two options I was going with.

"I don't think they meant to leave it there for us to find."

"Is this the moon monster's doing?" Garret questioned. I noticed a smerk form on his face. I ignored his attempt to play the situation down.

"Look," I said. "As a scientist, I like to deal with evidence from which I can form reasonable conclusions, but none of what happened on our walk leads me anywhere with great satisfaction.

When you fell in the hole, I saw a shadow moving near you. It was a quick glimpse, but it was there long enough to catch my eye and register in the back of my brain, and after the shadow vanished, the silver material was on the back of your legs Garret, and on the trail as well." I paused to observe the effect my words had upon Garret. His smile was gone and he looked concerned, but I had no idea if his concern was for my mental health or what he thought I thought had transpired. "And that's why I wanted to leave immediately," I concluded.

"I'm still not sure about all of this, so why don't we go back and check the area out. It should be safe. I mean they were all around us according to you, and they didn't harm us." Garret looked as if he wasn't even sure if he believed his own words. "Besides that so-called tunnel that I fell into might be worth looking into."

"I guess what I just said would be hard to believe unless you saw it for yourself." I acquiesced.

"And if we do run into someone or something?" Dean asked inquisitively, stressing his last word in a high-pitched tone.

"I wouldn't worry too much if I were you."

"That's reassuring." Garret replied. "It seems to me that I was the one in danger last time. So I'll let you drop into the tunnel first this time."

I laughed and told Garret, "Ok, I'll go down first, but do you mind if I use my feet to land on? I don't think my backside is as cushioned as yours!" Garret's face and ears turned red while Dean bust out laughing.

"That's enough you two, how about buying a drink for the mentally injured?"

"I'd be delighted, any particular number?" I said while trying to maintain his composure.

"Anything but 49-A," Garret groaned. Dean laughed and stated, "I found out that 49-A consists of scotch and concentrated green melon liquor."

"Sounds awful! But it tastes alright." I said as I reached for the buttons in the middle of the table and quickly pressed a sequence of buttons and leaned back in my chair.

"So what did you order?" Dean asked.

"Numbers 3-27-L."

"And what the heck does that stand for?" Garret asked, trying not to think of the possible consequences of a deadly hangover in the morning.

"That stands for three gin and tonics with a slice of lemon on the side. I think I'm getting the hang of this." The box descended back into the middle of the table. Then after a moment of silence, the box raised back up with three glasses filled with liquid in its center compartment. I sat and watched with a very pleased expression on my face. We reached for the glasses, sniffed at the contents just to make sure, and then took a sip.

"You make a mean gin and tonic." commented Garret. At this statement we all chuckled and began talking once again about everything under the sun. A few hours had passed and I was both intoxicated and hungry. As a matter of fact, we were all hungry. So we decided to leave the bar and visit the nearest food outlet. Normally I didn't drink so much, but this was my vacation and I was determined to indulge. We finally decided on pizza, partly because we all seemed to like it, and partly because the pizzeria was the first thing we found.

"Are you going to leave us so soon for your rendezvous?" Garret sarcastically asked. I looked up from the white tray of pizza, my mind blank with nothing to say.
"Oh come now. We're not naive," Garret, added, "If you meet her tonight make sure you wipe off the lipstick before you see us again. After all, there is no need to rub it in our faces." I shook my head and smiled. Then I remembered something they could find useful.

"I'll tell you what. Go to the reservation counter and ask where you might find a woman by the name of Cynthia. I think that she may be able to help you." Dean looked at me and responded with a warm light sparkling in his eyes.

"I hope your not just pulling our legs." Garret said suspiciously.

"I thought you two were the ones who played the practical jokes!"

"Well, we'll see." Garret wistfully said with a far away look. His mind was racing with the thought of encountering women at Expom and on another planet for that matter. He knew his wife would be busy doing whatever it was that she did, and tonight was just as good as any other night to fool around. Dean on the other hand was a little more conservative. He knew that his marriage was not as good as it had been in the past, but without the encouragement of Garret, he probably would never had had enough nerve to think of cheating on his wife. Garret had said that he brought out devil in him, but Dean liked his new outlook on life, at least until the relationship with his wife improved. So for the time being they would be the best of buddies and an indispensable cruising duo.

"I think I'll be turning in now," I yawned for effect as I pushed my chair away from the table and stood up.

"I hope the two of you enjoy the rest of the evening," I said.

"Whatever." Garret replied. Did they know something that I didn't know, or were they just trying to keep me in suspense? I figured that it was most likely the latter of the two possibilities. I said good night one last time, and then exited the bar.

"That was rather generous of him." Dean said as he watched me pass out through the doorway.

"We'll see about that!"

"For Heaven's sake, don't be such a pessimist! Besides your the one that should be encouraging me, not the other way around."

A look of surprise crossed Garret's face and he actually became amused. He suddenly felt like an electrical current had just passed through his body and he couldn't help cheer, "You're right, what are we waiting for?"

I went back to my room and was disappointed by finding it to be empty. Although I was tired and the pizza had upset his stomach, I still wanted to spend some time with Andrea.

"Oh well," I half mumbled to myself, "I guess I could use a full night's rest." With this depressing thought in mind I prepared to go to bed. I stripped off my clothes and slipped in between the cool sheets. As I lay there looking up at the dull finish of the ceiling, I thought about the day's events. Soon my thoughts turned to what the Russians had said. They had also witnessed shadows and they too had come into contact with the silver substance. The probability of such a coincidence was astronomical. There had to be a reason for all of this, and I was determined to find out what it was. Soon, however, sleep dissipated all thoughts for the night.

In the morning I woke to the sound of my own private alarm clock. I disliked the intercom system and found my own alarm to be more soothing on my nerves. However, I still rather quickly jumped out of bed as the alarm beeped. I rapidly got dressed in my dark blue and white jogging suit, slipped on my tennis shoes, and left the room. I wanted to arrive at the locker room early enough to check out my equipment and make sure that Dean and Garret hadn't had enough time to prepare a practical joke for me. I still didn't trust them completely after witnessing what they had done to the Russian official. I was indeed the first person there, so I proceeded with a thorough check of my gear. I found everything to be in order. At that moment Garret came in and headed straight for me.

"Where's your other half?" I asked him.

"He should be along soon. Man do I feel awful."

"And why is that?"

"We took your advice and went to see Cynthia." My curiosity couldn't let me resist asking him why.

"And what happened?"

"She wasn't there, but a couple of women sitting in the lounge kept us busy all night." I chuckled.

"I really feel sorry for you then!" As if on cue, Dean entered the room. It was the first time that I had not heard him shout out "Hello" as his usual greeting. He actually quietly said "Good morning" and walked towards his locker. Without another word spoken he started slowly pulling on his outdoor tour suit.

"He looks worse than I feel," Garret chuckled. Then he too began to don his suit. I was ready to go three minutes before they were. As a matter of fact, we were almost the very last to finish suiting up out of the entire group, and for a brief moment we feared that we would miss the tour completely if Dean failed to get his helmet placed correctly.

There were over thirty people on the tour. I figured that it would be relatively easy to break away from the main group once we reached the entrance of the moon cave. We sat in the back of the last shuttle bus and watched the familiar scenery flow past us as the bus sped down the rail. When it stopped, we made our way to the front, before we all started down the stairs. Once we were ahead of the lead guide in the moon cave, we turned down the passageway. I took one final glance behind me and yelled, "Lets go!"

The three of us began to run down the passage as well as anyone can be expected to run on the moon and turned the next corner with a sort of kangaroo hoping motion that we seemed to be perfecting with each stride. The forward tour guide had just turned the first corner in time to see the dust settling back down to the ground.

"Where did they go?" she muttered to herself.

"What did you say, Susan?" came a voice over her headphone.

"Oh nothing, I thought I saw three tourists go ahead of me, and now I don't see them!"

"Don't worry, they know the way. I recognized them from the tour yesterday. They'll probably show up at the great hall."

"Ok," Susan reluctantly replied.

The three of us had been running hard for the past several minutes. We were all rapidly becoming fatigued, but not one of us would be the first to admit it. Finally Dean could take no more.

"For God's sake, can't we take a break?" he managed to say between deep gapping breaths. We all stopped and laughed and tried to catch our breath at the same time.

"I think that we're far enough away to walk it from here," I said as I caught my breath and started to relax a little.

"I'm getting too old for this type of stuff," Garret complained.

"Are you alright Dean?" I asked as he tried to adjust the input sound volume on his helmet in order to quiet the harsh breathing sound from the two of us in his ears.

"Yeah, let's hit the road."

We walked the rest of the way and when we reached the point where we had diverted from the main trial, we adjusted our helmet lights and pulled the trail boundary rope slowly up over our heads. We were a bit more cautious this time, not knowing what to fear or what to expect that lay ahead of us.

As we walked down the side tunnel I spotted a few pieces of the silver material. We paused briefly to examine the material while I placed a piece into a small plastic bag that I had brought along. I had originally brought the bags to illegally collect some moon rock samples, but this was by far a more useful purpose.

"Why you old devil," Garret exclaimed. "You came prepared to take some souvenirs!"

"Only in the name of science." I stoically stated.

"In the name of science my ass," Dean interjected.

"You can't blame a guy for trying!"

"What do you plan on doing with that silver junk?" Garret asked.

"First of all I'm going to take it to the science officer on duty at the information center." By now I had wrapped the bag that contained the sample into a tight roll and had inserted it inside another bag and sealed it shut.

"That ought to keep the air out."

"Do you think that's why my sample disappeared?" Dean asked.

"What the air? . . . could be, but I'm not taking any chances."

Garret motioned forward and we began walking down the tunnel.

"This has got to be the spot!" We had walked down the tunnel almost to the end and still the site of our accident and the hole we helped create was nowhere to be found. There was no mistaking the tunnel. The cave in had to be here, but needless to say, it was gone. I flashed my light beam on the ground and could not tell if it had ever been disturbed. I kicked the dirt to reveal the lighter colored layers, all appeared to be normal.

"I think that whoever covered up the hole was extremely good at their craft."

"I can't believe it. Why would they do it?" Garret questioned as he began to jump up and down to try to break through the ground. Dean and I passively watched. The stomping on the ground only raised the dust and produced a hollow thumping sound.

"Stop for a minute," I said. "Do you hear that hollow sound?"

"Yeah," Dean replied as he began kicking at the dirt to reveal whatever was underneath. He had gouged a hole over five inches deep and still no sign of anything. "I'll need a shovel to dig this up." He was breathing heavily again, and he was tired of kicking at the soil. Garret never did hear the thumping noise that he had created, for his helmet was already pressing against his ears, and with every bounce the outside noise became obscured.

"Whoever covered this up had a purpose in mind," I added. "And I don't think that they'll appreciate it if we dig it back open."

"There must be a sheet of steel under there to resist my jumping because it wasn't this strong the day I fell in."

"You might be right Garret, I wouldn't doubt that it has been reinforced, but then again, you only weigh about forty pounds up here."

"What now," Dean asked.

"First I'm going to show this sample to Dr. Slatski and then I'm going to have another game of moon ball. Do either of you want to join me?"

"We'd like too, but our wives found out that we were enjoying ourselves so much that they decided that we were going to spend the afternoon with them." Garret mournfully wailed. I chuckled to myself as I had long since forgotten about such obligations that married life demanded.

"I'll let you know what Dr. Slatski says."
The three of us reluctant moon walkers started up the main trial, retracing our path. We could hear the group approaching. As the tour group moved into sight, we stood at the side of the path to fall in later at the end of the procession. The tour guides said nothing as they passed by. I thought that that was rather nice of them considering how rudely we had run off in the first place. I still felt bad for having caused the guides concern, but wasn't that what being a guide was all about? Tourist running off and getting lost or even worse, injured? Definitely not a job for one who wasn't patient or understanding I thought.

Back at the locker room, none of the attendants noticed as I transferred the plastic bag to the pocket of my pants. I told Dean and Garret goodbye and was once again off to see Dr. Slatski.

"For his sake, I hope his mood has improved," I muttered to myself as I made my way through the maze of corridors.

Dr. Slatski was in the office, and as usual, he was hunched over the table looking at a computer screen. I stepped through the door and once again he quickly clicked to a new screen. This struck me as being odd, for what was so important that he had to hide it every time someone entered the room?

"And how are you? Dr. Wilson," came the soft-spoken voice, "And what may I do for you today?" He had obviously changed his mood I noticed.

"I have something that I think you might find interesting." I paused for a second to see if the facial expressions of Dr. Slatski would change, but much to my disappointment they did not.

"And what is it?"

I pulled the bag containing the silver material out of my pocket and laid it on the desk. Dr. Slatski eyed the bag and asked nonchalantly, "Where did you get this?"

"I found it in the moon cave."

"You know that your not permitted to remove anything, don't you?" I was annoyed by this petty question and simply stood and looked at him.

"Certainly I can't tell anything by just looking at it. So why don't you stop in later. By then I will have had time to run an analysis."

"Does it even look familiar to you?"

Dr. Slatski leaned back in his chair with his arms crossed and contemplated the question before he spoke.

"I've seen over a dozen substances that look just like this." He picked up the bag and quickly let it fall through his fingers back onto the table. The motions were quick, but long enough for me to sense that he was indeed familiar with the material and for some reason he wanted nothing to do with it.

"There are probably over a million different materials that are scattered about on the surface of the moon. They have fallen as dust particles attracted by the gravitational field of the moon or they come in the form of meteors that have bombarded the moon over the past eons. With all of this input, I would be hard pressed to define and describe every type of material found here. So you see what I'm up against?"

"I appreciate your text book trivia of the moon, but nevertheless I will return later to see what you have found."

I was mad at this pompous man who treated me as a high school dropout and who would undoubtedly do nothing constructive with my sample. I headed for the door, but before I left the room, I turned and said, "By the way, one of those ground fissures sealed itself up. Do you know anything about that?"

Dr. Slatski looked at me coldly, "No, how would I?" The words were measured but stern.

"Very well then, I'll see you later." The minute I was sure he couldn't see me, I sneaked back down the hall as I dare without him seeing me.

Dr. Slatski picked up the bag as if to examine it. He opened the seal and laid the bag back down. He sat back in his chair feeling relieved of the entire situation. If he thought he could contain my persistence until I was due to return to Earth, he was dead wrong. Dr. Slatski tried to clear his mind by watching the slight movement inside the bag. The material had already begun to change from its jelly like structure to a colorless almost clear powder. He definitely knew what it was.

Page 112

As I headed in the direction of the moon ball courts, I thought about the mysterious Dr. Slatski; certain aspects did not quite fit. First of all, a scientist was generally very enthusiastic and would try to supplant their interest in a field into those that were near them. Also, they would perceive something considered to be mundane and uninteresting, and turn it into something useful in order to study and share their newfound knowledge with those that did not have their current level of knowledge. Both the ability to share and encourage seemed to be lacking in this so-called Dr. Slatski, and I had a hard time coping with the fact that this was the type of person that I would have to depend on for most of my information. Now, moon ball seemed more than just a form of exercise, but a method of releasing my pent up frustrations.

I entered the moon ball facility and found it to be relatively deserted. Most of the Expom guests were still engaged in guided tours and other activities. The dressing room was empty, so with no other people in my way, I quickly changed into red shorts and a loose weave white tank top and headed for one of the many unused courts. I settled on one that I had played in before. All the courts were exactly alike, but I felt psychologically at home in this one. Humans are, after all, creatures of habit. Standing in the middle of the court, I began with some warm up shots before I would eventually tackle some of the advanced moves that I had witnessed Jason using. Already I felt more comfortable with my newfound lack of weight. The ball still felt slippery to the touch. At least that's what I told myself each time when I lost control of the direction in which the ball traveled. Another five minutes and the ball seemed to move more on demand and less erratic. I was soon perspiring profusely. Even with the reduced gravity, the game was a total work out. Over compensating for where one would normally lean, jumping higher in order to utilize the ceiling, and using one's side muscles to cushion the crashing into the walls and floor in order to save a shot at the last possible moment. I was not alone in his game. Above in the spectator stands stood a figure silently looking down at me through a dark plastic screen. The figure stood for quite some time before I had the opportunity to glance upward and detect the faint outline pressing against the observation window.

"Hello," the figure yelled down. I recognized the voice as Jason's.

"Care to have another game?" I shouted back at him.

"I wish I could, but I don't have the time right now. I have another lovely meeting to go to."

"What type of work do you do?" I asked as I hit the ball against the far wall. I figured that I could talk and get in a few rounds at the same time. However, I soon found that this was almost impossible for one so new to the game.

"I'm in Engineering, but this guy from the government insisted that all of us be at the meeting." I could almost visualize the disgusted look on Jason's face.

"His name isn't Bill Nico by chance is it?" Jason was surprised by this unexpected question.

"Yes, but how did you know?"

"We flew over together to Flagstaff from Hawaii."

"Then are you here for the same reason?"

"Not exactly," I literally had no idea why Bill Nico was here, but I thought I would at least see how much I could find out. The name had been a lucky guess, primarily because Bill was the only government official that I knew at Expom at the present time.

"What sort of questions has he been asking you?" I continued.

"Well, we're not suppose to talk about it, but since you already know him, I guess it's ok." He took a deep breath while he collected his thoughts. "When we lost those two cargo shipments, I guess they got pretty mad at us." I stopped suddenly in mid swing. This was going to be more interesting than I had first imagined.

"Wait a minute Jason, let me come up there and you can tell me the whole story from the beginning." I ran out of the court and up to the balcony. I had no idea what Jason was talking about, but with all that had happened to me so far, I had to see if any of it was related. "Well, let's hear your version from the top," I said to Jason as I reached the top of the stairway. We both sat down on one of the benches and Jason began his story.

"I first noticed something was going on about two years ago when we began losing tools and minor things. Then when those two shipments came to Expom and the next day they were gone, I really got baffled. I mean it's impossible for anything to walk
off and be missing here on the moon? There's no place to go."

"I see," I was thinking the same thing myself.

"No one could figure it out. One day the parts were there, the next day they were gone, and the cargo story gets even better. No one even knows who ordered the stuff, and when it got here, no one knows what happened to it."

"Do you know what the contents of the cargo were?" I asked.

"They won't tell us anything, except that two cargo containers are missing."

"That's pretty strange alright."

"Listen, I'm not in any trouble or anything like that am I?" Jason asked.

"Don't worry about it, but then again, don't tell anyone else about what we discussed. Ok?"

"Sure, no problem. I'd like to stay out of this as much as possible."

"I wouldn't want you to be late for your meeting, so I'll see you later." I noticed the nervous expression on Jason's face.

"Not about this. I want another chance at beating you at this crazy game." I smiled and remained seated as Jason got up and left the balcony. Something was going on here and I was intrigued. I knew it had to include the shiny material, the shadows, Dr. Slatski, and the missing cargo. I definitely lost interest in moon ball. I decided that it was time to go back to my room and make a call to Dan Crutino back at M.B.I.: The Marine Biology Institute.

Back at my room, I sat in front of the screen waiting for the picture to visualize. When the screen finally lit up, Dan's face appeared. He looked rather sleepy with his eyes barely opened and his face unshaven, but this didn't bother me. The two of us had been best friends at one point in our careers and now we at least respected one another enough to long since do away with formal protocols.

"Listen Dan, I've come across some things up here that I'd like to have checked out. They have apparently lost some cargo shipments, and I think it's connected to traces of some silver substance that I've found up here. I think I could find where the cargo went if I could use of the D.T.V. unit." The DTV unit was used in deep sea trench scouting. The unit stood about two feet tall, had six small wheels attached to two rubber tracks, and could basically fit in the back of a pickup truck including an array of detachable six foot long arms for used for sampling and removing things from the Ocean's substrate. The unit had one camera eye located in the center that could look 360 degrees, and two arms with claws, could hang from the front and backside of the unit. All this and the fact that it was experimentally nuclear powered, led me to believe that it would be perfect for scouting on the moon.

"You want me to do what?" came the high-pitched voice on the other end of the line.

"Look, talk to your government friends and tell them that I'm willing to help an NSA agent named Bill Nico, if I can have the D.T.V. up here"

"I sure hope you know what you're doing," Dan said as he yawned.

"Yes I'm positive, just let me know what the answer is soon."

"Ok," came the reply as Dan's face faded from the screen.

"That ought to stir things up," I said to the dark screen. I didn't really intend on finding any cargo, but it was a good way to get my equipment up to Expom, so I could at least investigate the moon caves. Stolen or misplaced cargo could always be replaced, and to me it was far more important to try and satisfy my curiosity, and leave the theft detection work to people like Mr. Nico.

As I sat in my chair thinking about how I would utilize the DTV unit, my front door slid open, followed by the entrance of Andrea.

"Hello," She smiled and then came over to me and gave me a very sensuous kiss that lasted for what seemed like several minutes. I immediately forgot about the DTV unit and anything else for that matter. She felt so good in my arms. She was simply irresistible I thought. She brought out primitive emotions that lay deep within me, emotions that I would have denied the possibility of possessing if she had not brought them to my foremost attention. These emotions were not entirely new, for they had been evoked during the span in my life when my wife was still alive. After her death, those feelings fled deep within my soul and although those feelings could have been aroused, I buried myself so far beneath my work, that they had little chance to let themselves be known. Now those sensations seemed unfamiliar and I found it hard to cope with them. Yet, I desired to kiss her, to touch her, and completely enrapture her with what I at first thought was love, but I knew I had to resist these temptations. I did not want to risk either becoming too emotionally involved if I could help it, or the thought of suffocating her with so much closeness that would in turn drive her away from me. It was not so much her, as a person that attracted me, but her physical presence and the ability to share my emotions with someone. I had realized after we had met that I was fond of her, but in love with the act of being in love itself. As to what she thought of me, I could only guess. She at least enjoyed being with me, I surmised.

"Did you enjoy your tour?" she asked as she leaned away from me in order to catch her breath and straighten her attire.

"The tour was fine." I rose out of my chair and placed my arms around her. I began to kiss her passionately. She seemed to enjoy it, but suddenly stopped me.

"I know what you have in mind, but I am just dying for something to eat," she said as she backed away from my embrace.

"My apologies. Would you like to join me for dinner?"

"That would be nice, but I would like to stop by my place first and change." I noticed that she was still wearing her blue Expom Company uniform. Although the uniform resembled the nostalgic retro Pan American World Airlines Flight Attendant uniform, against her body, she made the lines look more like they belonged on a one of a kind designer outfit.

"Of course. Shall I wait for you here or accompany you to your place?"

"I think I could get more accomplished if you waited here," she said with a stern composure that lasted only seconds before breaking into a giggle. "I'll be back within an hour." She kissed me a few more times and then left the room.

I wore a very smug expression as I thought about what the evening had in store for me. I also felt twenty years younger. I didn't take long to shower, shave, and dress in appropriate evening clothes. When I was finished I sat in front of the video monitor, waiting for Andrea to walk through the door.

Finally the doorbell rang, but she did not enter, so I got out of my chair and headed towards the door. As I neared the door however, the sensor was activated and it opened. There in front of me stood Bill Nico.

"May I have a word with you Dr. Wilson?" came his harsh, angry voice. I was immediately disappointed that it was not Andrea; and at the same time quite surprised to see Bill so soon.

"Sure come on in," I said, although Bill had already entered.

"Not here, I have something to show you. Would you come with me Dr. Wilson?"

"Call me John, and can't it wait until tomorrow?" I impatiently asked.

"No, the sooner the better."

"You realize that you're going to ruin my evening!"

"Can't be helped John."

"Alright, let's get this over with then," I sort of grumbled while conjuring up the most menacing glare I could to throw in Bill's direction.

"I received a message concerning you," Bill began as we made our way out of the room. I walked along in silence, wondering if this wouldn't take too long. "I was going to see you later on this week anyway, but you seem to have advanced my time schedule."

"What did you want to see me about?" I was sure that the two of us had nothing on Earth in common, and probably not so much up here at Expom either.

"I'll explain everything in cargo bay Delta." For the rest of the distance we walked in silence.

The door opened to the cargo bay Delta and the lights automatically turned on. Inside the huge room stood mostly boxes piled on pallets. Some of them had stickers on the side with final destinations marked with a green tag for "Earth", and others with red tags for "Expom". We were alone in the room, and it gave me an eerie feeling.

"I'm not sure how you found out," Bill continued. "But I was going to use you anyway."

"What do you mean by that?" I was truly surprised. Bill ignored the tone of my voice.

"We already have a model similar to your D.T.V. unit on site. As a matter of fact, it's inside that crate." He pointed to a large crate sitting near us. "You were brought up here to operate it if need be." I was mad now, really angry. The company had conspired against me, and I knew I couldn't refuse even if I wanted to. Bill noticed my expression and spoke up quickly. "It wasn't suppose to sound like an order, but you broadcasted that cargo was missing, over the video screen, and we have no idea who may be monitoring those transmissions. Therefore, we have to assume that it was monitored, and hope that we can still catch them slightly off guard."

"Catch who off guard?" I felt disbelief and detachment welling up inside me like a cold current with every piece of new information this crazy government agent was dishing out.

"We're not sure, some speculate the Russians, and some think that it might be another hostile entity. You see we don't even have a clue as to who is behind it, and the missing cargo is of vital concern to U.S. interests. Some of the material is highly classified. How it ended up going to Expom is still another mystery. There has to be someone here working on the inside, but we have no suspects, and everyone working here appears clean."

"Even Dr. Slatski?" I asked out of curiosity. Bill raised his brows and answered.
"We've already checked him out. He hasn't received or sent one transmission in over a year, and that's where the problem lies. We have proof that the material was requested here and sent here, but none of it has left here. So, logic dictates that it would be stored here some place. Yet we don't have a clue where to find it or who requested it"

"And you already decided to use the probe to find it?"

"Well, the answer is simple, if we brought an army up here to search for where the material is hidden, then the entire world would eventually learn what has happened. This would of course embarrass the entire NATO alliance. However, if we use your probe, we can do the investigating quite unobtrusively. The DTV unit can do the work of twenty skilled men and does not stick out like a sore thumb; It's simply another lunar mechanical toy."

"When do you want me to start operating it?" I sighed and suddenly felt very weary.

"Would you believe right now?" That's exactly what I thought he would say.

"What? I don't see any reason to start right now, why we can't start tomorrow. After my date, you get the picture?" Although I rather doubted he would.

"We have over a ton of plutonium stacked neatly in the next cargo bay. I believe it's Bay Epsilon. I expect it to be stolen by tomorrow morning lunar time. Now what I plan on doing, is to have your unit set up and ready to observe them in the act and record the event for later prosecution. If we catch them red handed and follow them, we may not have to spend a lot of time on our own trying to find the rest of the missing cargo."

"This is going to take a lot of time. So do you mind if I at least cancel my dinner date? I demanded, my voice rising with each word.

"Out of the question. The fewer the number of people that know what we are, or are not doing, the better."

"You certainly don't know much about women and what I'll have to try and explain later!"

"I'll try and make it up to you," Bill grinned and slapped me on the shoulder. We walked over to a crate that had colorful Marine Biology Institute stickers covering its sides.

"By the way, was it just a coincidence that you were on my flight?" I asked.

"I'm afraid I can't answer that."

"Just as I thought." Bill pressed several buttons on the side of a crate and the side facing us lowered down to form a ramp. On the bottom of the ramp was a control box strapped to the ramp by velcro. I reached down and released the box from the straps. Next I raised the control box to chest level and activated the DTV unit. After pressing several buttons, the probe began moving out of the crate. Immediately I noticed that the rubberized tank tracks had been enlarged and modified for better surface traction on the moon. I pressed the main power button while it was still in the crate and slowly maneuvered the DTV down the ramp. I could see that they had made modifications to the battery units too. All other aspects of the DTV unit appeared normal and operational. Nevertheless, I examined it and tested every function to see if any other changes had been made. We walked the unit into the adjacent cargo room and then the two of us returned to cargo bay Delta. Bill explained to me how he had set up an off line video screen from the main terminal and how we could use it to monitor the plutonium. I connected the control box in line with the video screen, made a few last minute adjustments, and all was ready.

Page 125

The viewing screen was the only light source in the small cubical room. Infrared red light poured over the two of us as we were sitting silently in our chairs. Bill was calm, methodical, and patiently waiting to ensnare his prey in the prepared trap. My eyes were mere slits becoming thinner until I could hardly focus on the screen. I was totally bored and almost in a hypnotic state from five hours of watching a cargo bay devoid of life. As my eyelids finally shut, the opening of the outer bay doors activated the noise monitor; darkness still prevailed so all would appear normal to the intruders. Within fractions of a second, figures walked by the front of the screen. Using the infrared monitor, I could only make out their outer bodylines and the shape of the helmets that they wore.

As I began pressing buttons, color images of bright red, yellow, and blue hues appeared on the screen. Yet the fixed monitors located in the cargo bay would as usual detect nothing out of the norm. I continued pushing buttons back and forth several times to make sure that the images were correct. I happened to look back, hearing noises behind me, and saw Bill fully dressed in a moon suit with a specially designed shotgun straddled across his left arm. He had an insidious out of character grin on his face as if he were possessed or a like crazed hunter going out for the kill.

"Are you out of your mind? You're not going to arrest them like that, are you?"

"Why not?" Bill simply stated.

"For one thing, they're not human!"

"What?" Bill was sure that I had lost my marbles." I pointed at the screen.

"Look at the screen," I said.

"This is the imagery using the heat scanner."

"So," Bill said still speculating my state of mind.

"Humans wearing spacesuits do not put out that kind of heat signature!"

Bill lowered his gun as he continued to scrutinize the figures portrayed on the screen.

"You know that cargo Bay Epsilon cannot be pressurized with the outer door opened, so how thick do you think their spacesuits are?"

Bill looked at the screen even more intensely. The helmets that they wore appeared to be disproportionably large compared to the rest of their faintly outlined bodies.

"Those suits aren't ours, so I guess for now I won't go in there and break up their party."

"Not until we know if they are carrying weapons." Bill looked down at the brightly polished gun, like a child who just had his favorite toy belittled and admonished.

"You think I'm bringing a knife to a gun fight?"

"I think nothing less."

Bill didn't hear me, for he had returned his attention to concentrating on the thieves. The two of us sat and watched as the silent silhouettes did their assigned tasks.

"They don't even utter a word," Bill said.

"Do you see how highly organized they work, like a single unit."

One of the figures finally stopped. It seemed to be taking a break with its back directly in front of the lens. I punched several buttons and the probe shot forward from its hiding spot. My aim was good and the probe hit the figure in the right side of its body as the figure turned to see what was making the noise. The DTV unit stopped on impact at the point of impact. The blurred figure moved out of view.

"That should shake them up a little." I couldn't believe it but the lens had a crack along the front of the glass with a greasy substance smeared across it as well, which made half of the screen blurred.

"There goes the lens." I barely got the word out when bolt of light flashed in front of the screen and turned the screen dark."

"Now you've done it. They know that we know about them.

"Perhaps, but now that they know they are being watched they might just make a fatal mistake." Just then we saw a bright light hit the doors that opened up into cargo bay Epsilon.

"They just welded our doors shut. I guess they still want to keep to themselves." The lights abruptly went off in our cargo bay.

"On the bright side we are still alive," I said.

"Yes, but for how long?"

"You tell me."

"Well, I guess I could go back and report that alien's stole the plutonium, I'll lose my job and probably be sent to an insane asylum. However, if I try and arrest them?"

"You might be flashed like the DTV," I interjected.

"Is that your official scientific opinion?"

"It's obvious that they don't want anything to do with us and they might have been here before us, so I think that we had better just leave it at that, unless the DTV is still usable enough to follow their tracks outside?"

"No, that won't be necessary," Bill, replied. I looked at him rather oddly.

"Does this mean that you're giving up on the investigation?"

"No, I just know that there won't be any tracks to follow. This isn't the first time that I have tried to find where the missing cargo has gone; then again, I think I will take a brief walk around the premises. It might do me some good. You can come too if you like."

"No thanks," I said. " But could you also check on the DTV once the doors are repaired. As long as you think it'll be safe, I think I'll go have a word or two with Dr. Slatski."

"Sure. I appreciate your help," Bill added. "However, if you think he's involved, he should be considered dangerous too, so be careful."

"I'll try and keep that in mind." I had a difficult time keeping a straight face as I said this. Bill didn't even seem to catch the sarcasm in my voice. Bill reminded me exactly of the government guys I read about in fiction spy novels; from the lack of a sense of humor, to the dark blue suit, and the dark sunglasses. I'm surprised he wasn't wearing sunglasses right now. The lights suddenly came back on.

Page 131

I proceeded directly to the Information Center. The room was unlocked, yet Dr. Slatski was nowhere in sight. I made his way over to the desk to have a seat and wait. The surface of the desk had been cleared off, and was unnaturally neat. My thoughts turned to the papers that Dr. Slatski had constantly been reshuffling and hiding from other's view. Instead of sitting down like I had originally planned, I decided to see if I could find the papers and see why they were so important.

As I made my way around the desk I saw that the drawers all had internal locks on them. I glanced around the room for something to use to pry them open. I found several suitable objects, but only one proved to be suitable; the switchblade knife that I had illegally smuggled to Expom. I kept it with me at all times. The knife was intrinsically part of me for it was the one last possession that I had retained from a period in my life when I was young and still not set in any definite cast or course of career. The our inch blade that I had protracted was blemished from oils and resins made contact with over the years of perpetual abuse. The thin blade easily worked its way through the circular lock and within seconds the drawer opened. The whole process reminded me of an old James Bond film, the type that had long since been forgotten by history.

I rapidly shuffled through the papers, but I didn't find anything of any consequences, then I noticed that the note paper pad hand something on it. Holding it up to the light I could see the imprint of the words "cargo bay Epsilon", and a door code. I took the top piece of paper and put it in my pocket and set the note pad back on the desk just as I had found it. I had just finished placing my knife back in my pocket when Dr. Slatski entered the room.

I knew the doctor was surprised to see me standing behind his desk, but he managed to keep the expression on his face extremely neutral.

"Dr. Wilson, I'm surprised to see you so soon."

"I imagine you are." Dr. Slatski gave me a sudden out of place look, then he promptly dismissed whatever he was thinking and continued talking in a soft toned voice.

"I haven't had time to run an analysis on that sample yet."

"Never mind about that, I already found what it was connected to on my own."

"Oh?" Dr. Slatski asked as he unsteadily sat down in his chair. "And what did you find out?"

"I think you already know."

"I'm afraid that I don't understand." Dr. Slatski twisted a pen back and forth between his fingers, and from time to time glanced at me. His lips were drawn in tightly and his eyes were squinted into thin lines. Would he attack me here and now I wondered? I was certain that I could defend myself, from Dr. Slatski. He was smaller in size and not very muscular, but I had no idea whether or not he was armed.

"Well, are you going to tell me?" Dr. Slatski's voice sounded more like a command than a simple question. I felt a little uneasy as to the way this meeting was progressing, but I had to continue.

"Dr. Slatski, do you believe in aliens?" Dr. Slatski sat passively trying to once again get a grip on his emotions.

"I don't see why not, but what does this have to do with the sample?"

"I think you not only believe in them, but I think that you know for a fact that they exist!"

"Really? And what makes you come to such a ridiculous conclusion?" Dr. Slatski shook his head in disappointment, hoping that this would end this unbelievable conversation. Unfortunately I would not be put off so easily.

"I don't know why, but I do know for a fact that you are indeed helping them."

"You must be mad!" Dr. Slatski rose out of his chair and shouted at me. He realized how brash his actions had been and tried to calm himself by pacing the narrow confines of the room. I stood silently and patiently waited for him to continue speaking. My stare seemed to be agitating him further. A cold tingle of premonition ran down my spine and made the hairs on the back of my neck rise. For some strong feeling I suddenly felt vulnerable.

"You can't be serious about this? Besides, how could you ever prove such a thing?"

"I have the proof. I don't want to make it public, at least not at this point in time. I'm a scientist; my main goal is simply to learn who they are, and why you are helping them. I need to fulfill my curiosity, nothing more at this time." This seemed to relax Dr. Slatski, for he ceased pacing his narrow path and his face took on a less aggravated appearance. He took a deep breath while he looked up at the ceiling.

"Dr. Wilson, suppose you found another life form. Suppose they were next to death or helpless. Would you try to save them or would you let them die?"

"Provided they weren't bent on destroying mankind I would try to save them."

"You might at that, but do you think that the rest of mankind would feel the same way?" I hesitated as I thought of an appropriate answer.

"Just as I thought." Dr. Slatski broke the silence. "You don't know, and it's that chance that can't be taken. To make things more interesting, what if you knew that the other form of life was distantly related to man, but much more advanced? Do you think that mankind from Earth would openly welcome these aliens and accept their place as being found primitive, or shall I say, inferior to these aliens?" I didn't say anything. "I thought not!"

"Do you think that you can save them by letting them steal whatever they need without people becoming suspicious?"

I was beginning to think that this guy was incredibly naive.

"The plan has worked so far," the whisper was soft, but it reverberated off the walls. I felt the challenge behind the words.

"The government is presently investigating the missing cargo," I said.

Dr. Slatski sighed, his shoulders slumped and he slowly walked to his chair wiping his hand across his sweaty forehead.

Once seated, he was aware of a steady ache that was building behind his eyes, and this irritating man was the cause of it.

"It doesn't matter, the time is close at hand when they will be leaving."

"I would like to meet them before they go," I anxiously added.

"That may be arranged, now please discontinue your prying. Time is precious, and they can ill afford to cover every tunnel, nor watch your every move." I resented having the restriction placed upon me, but nodded my head in agreement. Silence ensued for a moment while we each evaluated the situation.

"Dr. Slatski, I have one other question that I'd like you to answer now."

"Alright, what is it?"

"How did you originally distinguish that they would not be aggressive towards you, and for that matter, the rest of mankind?"

"Instincts, purely instincts and nothing else. You know when you feel something is right; that it's a safe situation? That may not sound like a very scientific approach, but it turned out to be correct. Besides, they showed no aggression towards man before they became marooned here, so I see no reason for them to change their position afterwards. Especially after I have given them my help."

"Since it's obvious that you are communicating with them, what was their explanation for being marooned here in the first place, and why didn't they simply have their own kind to rescue them?" My mind raced as I formed preconceived solutions to my own questions.

"I can assure you that they were not running away from their own kind, when the accident occurred, if that's what your getting at, but I don't have enough time to give you further details. For now, you will have to trust me and I will have to trust you. It is possible that I may need your help if the aliens are to survive."

"Very well, if what you say is true, then I'll keep silent for the time being." I automatically stretched out my hand to Dr. Slatski. The doctor hesitated for a brief moment then firmly shook my hand. We were looking eye to eye. Suddenly, as our hands drew apart, my subconscious made me look down at the spot where their two hands had only just touched, but whatever thought promoted such a response was only there for a blink of the eye, and lost as Dr. Slatski spoke to me.

"Please be patient with us and I will explain it all to you very soon."

Page 138

I felt like I would burst with questions, but I was also exhilarated like any young child with a new, intriguing idea. My whistling could be heard throughout the corridor as I returned to my room. As the door slid open, I saw Bill Nico sitting in front of the monitor watching reruns of the first space missions on the guest services channel. Without hesitation I shouted at Bill's back, "Does everybody have a key to my room?"

"No, I think only that little lady Andrea and me." Bill replied in a matter-of-fact tone.

"She was here too?" I couldn't keep the excitement out of my voice.

"Yes, but I sent her away. Though I think she will return later."

"What!" I burst out, as both of my hands curled into tightly closed fists.

"Relax, she won't leave you until you return to Earth."

"Tell me how you can be so sure."

"It's her modus oporendi, one tourist per visit, some prefer more."

"I suppose you know her life history as well?"

"I have access to everybody's. Compared to her, you are a boy scout. Would you like a drink? I took the liberty of opening up your bar."

"Not at all, can I get you anything else now that I'm here in person?" I sarcastically asked through gritted teeth.

Bill feebly attempted to smooth things over by stating, "I think you could use a drink." He wasn't sure what I would find appealing, so he simply made what he liked and hoped that I would be receptive. I took the drink the agent handed to me; I looked at the contents, and immediately recognized it as scotch. Thoughts of late night sojourns in Tokyo began to make my stomach grumble, but that was a long time ago so I brought the peace offering to my lips and swallowed the fiery liquid. So much for swearing off scotch, I thought as I felt the bile rise in my throat. I glanced over at Bill who had returned to watching the space missions and decided the drink was as lousy as the company.

"Thanks, but I'm beginning to like the aliens a lot better than you." I disgustedly set my glass on the table.

"It's part of my job to rub people the wrong way. Have you talked with the aliens already?"

"No, not yet, but I do believe that I will soon."

"Let me know when you do," Bill whimsically began, "because if they are friendly, I'd like to ask them how I might be able to explain all of this to my superiors."

I could think of no other time when I felt so frustrated with another human being. In an attempt to cool off I made myself a new drink of dark Jamaican rum and diet coke, Expom style, which meant that the oval pieces of ice floated higher in the liquid than the cubes of ice would in the islands. As I sipped the refreshing tropical beverage, I challenged Bill.

"By the way, I'm taking tomorrow off, which means I'm not available for any of your investigative exploits."

"That fits in nicely with my plans too."

"What do you mean?"

"They have one more shipment destined for Expom two days from now. It's a container filled with advanced electronic gear, and like the cargo of plutonium, it doesn't belong here. I've been considering just canceling the entire shipment.

"You can't do that," I interrupted.

"Why not? Is there something that you're not telling me?" Bill looked inquisitively at me as he walked to the bar to pour himself another drink.

"No, nothing like that, I just want another chance to film and perhaps try to capture one of them." I had no such intents, but I had to stall Bill somehow. I realized that like Dr. Slatski, I too had become an accomplice to a race of creatures that I knew nothing about.

"Do you have a plan?"

"No, but I'll work on it."

"Very well, I'll approve the shipment, but remember, if you can't figure out a way, then you sure bet that I will." The look in Bill's eyes gave me an uneasy feeling, and I had no doubt that he would indeed find a way; maybe not the most pleasant way, but definitely an effective way.

"By the way, I received some more information from Washington. From what I have concluded, if anyone has the right to kill us, the aliens are prime candidates." I was stunned and looked at him in disbelief.

"What brings you to that conclusion?"

"It's just a theory of mine, but back in nineteen eighty-two we sent a military device called R.E.D.S. to the moon. Its mission was to land on the moon, aim a high-energy beam at a designated satellite, then self destruct. It was suppose to create the perfect malfunction. However, it landed hard and failed to operate properly. It was a test program that eventually was scuttled. The area where it was supposed to have landed is close by Expom, but when they searched for the device they found nothing. I went through some other records and came across an unexplained large explosion in this area two months after R.E.D.S. had been considered destroyed by the impact. It wasn't capable of creating an explosion of the magnitude recorded, so yet another question remained unsolved about the moon."

"So what does this have to do with the aliens?"

"The way I see it they have stolen enough equipment to make their own space craft. Now why would they need to build an entire spacecraft unless something happened to the one that they came in?" Bill paused for a moment and then continued. "Now my theory is that they found the damaged device and tried to fix it or something like that, and got themselves blown up when the detonator finally became operational."

My lower jaw dropped and I was speechless. Bill's theory sounded reasonable, but it led me to ask myself more questions than I could answer. I finally found my voice and asked, "If you're right, what do you plan on doing?"

"I want to bring them out in the open."

"What good will that do? They want as little to do with us as possible with us."

"You don't have to tell me that. I've read about UFO's all my life."

"Then why do you persist?"

"Because if the Russians meet them first, then they may try to take advantage of the situation." Bill vehemently replied.

"You can't be serious, they haven't helped them before, so what makes you think that they will have a change of heart in the future?"

"For one thing, it wasn't the Russians that nearly destroyed their entire crew." Bill was quite serious and some how in his twisted brain I believe he was determined to win them over to the American way. This, I was sure of.

"I hope that persuading them won't involve killing too many more of them!"

"No, nothing that extreme."

"You certainly haven't instilled a lot of confidence in me with what you've said so far." Bill shrugged his shoulders and looked directly at my blatantly annoyed face.

"I'm not concerned with what you believe. As long as you don't interfere with my plans, everything will run smoothly."

"I'll bet," I grumbled under my breath in order to prevent Bill from hearing. I decided to try new tactics to convince him to forget about the aliens. "If they were ready to meet us they would have already done so. Maybe they are just too advanced for us, and are waiting for us, as a race, to mature."

Bill became silent for a moment as he contemplated what I said. He turned off the video screen that he had been watching the old space mission reruns on, and gazed about the room with a frown that burrowed deep lines across his forehead and on both sides of his lips.

"I think I understand what you mean. You're thinking that if we can't even handle destructive items, such as nuclear weapons, then we certainly couldn't cope with anything more advanced?"

"That is precisely what I'm getting at. Among other things of course." I studied my drink as I swished the liquid around in the glass, causing the ice to crash and tumble. I liked to hear the musical tinkling it created, and I hoped it would annoy somehow annoy Bill. I continued thinking about the problem of trying to protect the aliens. As my thoughts turned more philosophical I commented, "however, there is a bright side to exposing them."

"This ought to be good coming from you," Bill snorted.

"I think it would be very difficult for racism to continue once humans realized that mankind as a whole was only one of a number of various life forms, and that it didn't matter if one was Black, Chinese, or Russian. We are all from the same planet and it's quite possible that the aliens see us all being the same." I chuckled and before Bill could ask me what was so amusing, I continued, "Wouldn't it be ironic if the aliens had their own prejudice system, and in that system we're at the bottom of the scale?"

"Oh, you mean the way Europeans first described people that they discovered in the Americas?"

"Well, that's not quite what I had in mind." I answered.

"Perhaps more like, while we fight among each other on Earth, the aliens might be looking down on us as we would a pack of dogs fighting over a bone, wondering to themselves why don't they just share?"

"They must be a patient race for letting us persist in our primitive ways. But I wonder how long their patience will last?" I stretched out my arms and yawned. "But I'm not going to worry about that tonight Bill. So if you will excuse me, I think I'll go get some sleep."

"I suppose you deserve it. I'll keep in touch so we can set something up before the next shipment arrives." Bill set his glass down on the table and sauntered out the door. I watched for the panel to slide closed behind him. I turned out the light, and fell on the bed fully dressed.

Page 146

I looked up at the ceiling. The room was pitch black, but I could still make out the pattern of the stucco. Sleep would not come easily this night. Too much had transpired in the space of one day for my mind to absorb and resolve. Too many questions had to be answered with no solutions in sight.

I had also been slightly disturbed by the situation with Andrea; Not that I disapproved of her life style, but whether or not I would see her again. My stomach began to growl and I realized that not only had Bill sent Andrea away, but he had also deprived me of eating anything for dinner. This was the last straw I thought. I got off the bed and straightened my clothes. I wasn't sure where I was going to go or what I was going to do, but I thought I would at least try and see what had happened to her.

I left the room and headed towards the reservation center. When I arrived, I noticed that the entire area was deserted. One single employee fought to keep awake as he swayed back and forth behind a podium like counter. He suddenly happened to see me out of the corner of his eye and he quickly came to attention. Someone to talk to the young man must have thought. His job, most likely, demanded long hours without anyone to talk to, so whenever the opportunity presented itself, he probably took full advantage of human interaction.

"Can I help you sir?" came a pleading voice. I was sure that this young man could in no way be of any service to me, but something inside made me willing to take the time and approach this very desperately lonely person.

"Are you enjoying your stay?" The young man said with relief as I approached him. I eyed him for a brief second, read his name badge, and then answered.

"Yes Erik, I'm looking for Andrea ... With a sinking feeling I realized I had forgotten her last name. As I tried to make my tongue bring forth the forgotten word, Erik seized the opportunity to speak.

"I believe I know who you are referring to. However I haven't seen her for almost two days." He said this with such wanton desire that I was sure that he thought more of her than just as a friend or a fellow company employee.

"Yes she is a beautiful woman isn't she?" The forwardness of my statement startled the young man and he tried to straighten his body as if the new position would improve the masking of his own personal feelings.

"I wish I could help you..." Erik trailed off. After pausing a moment, he smiled, "come with me". He moved down to the far end of the counter and opened a gate that led behind to where he was standing. "I'm in charge right now, so I'll let you come back to the operations center. A friend of Andrea is on duty right now, and if anyone knows where she is, this one will know."

I followed Erik as he went through one of the doors behind the counter. Behind the door, stairs led upward and around the corner. We passed through a set of doors, larger than the ones at the bottom of the stairs, and into the operations room. It was very large with the and filled with the faint hum of laser printer fans. The place had the smell of heated plastic, probably from years and years of running computers 24/7. There were about ten employees in all monitoring the place and from the looks of the empty desks, I could tell that the night shift was a bare bones skeleton crew. All of the workers appeared to have their hands busy, monitoring screens, or purposefully moving files on display from one place to another, collecting and disbursing various simulated cloud papers and forms. It looked like there was no room for slackers in this outfit, but then again, with the selection of applicants that were available to Expom, little else but the best work force could be expected.

"She might know." Erik blurted out boisterously. He pointed to a woman sitting in front of one of the many flat glass screens that were strewn around the room. Upon hearing the all too familiar voice, the woman cringed and reluctantly turned to face Erik. She was a very attractive woman. Long wavy black hair fell on her shoulders and stopped at the point where the tight fitting company uniform did little to hide her ample cleavage. I was in love at first sight. There was no end to what the women of Expom could do for an otherwise drab looking uniform. Even her long slender legs hidden behind the deep burgundy colored uniform demanded immediate respect. As if we were already half naked, and lying on the sands of a Fijian beach, my eyes slowly strayed back to her voluptuous cleavage. There was something about a woman's breast size that seemed to mesmerize me. Some men preferred legs, some preferred "buns", so that left all the rest for me. It was a happy arrangement respected and agreed upon by men of every background and culture. The woman was not only breathtakingly beautiful, but in order to hold such a position of responsibility, she would have to be very intelligent as well.

"What is it now?" she said in a quiet monotone voice as she refocused her eyes. She seemed to be annoyed by Erik's intrusion, but subdued her reactions as she noticed me man standing beside him. She thought that Erik talked too much.

Every time he entered the room he would have to be practically thrown out before he would leave. She realized, of course, that he had a lonely job, and because of this she occasionally tolerated his presence. To her it was one thing to talk when something of value was said, but quite another when the dialogue was meaningless, and this is where Erik excelled. He was lucky to have had relatives and connections, or a person of his caliber would have never set foot on Expom soil. She was certain of this fact.

"This man is looking for Andrea, and I thought you might be able to help him." Erik spoke the words as if he knew that every sound offended her and when he had finished, he stood patiently waiting for an approving gesture. I took this opportunity to introduce myself.

"My name is John."

"I'm Julie. Oh Erik, is anyone on duty downstairs?" A look of stark terror flashed on his face followed by a quick turn and the sound of feet pounding down the stairs.

"I'm not usually so gruff, he's a nice boy, but a bit mental. Now let's see, you wanted to find Andrea?"

"I did when I first came in here." I gave her a look of pure desire. She liked what I said, and even more the way my eyes seemed to penetrate deep within her. What she relished most was that she could still evoke the sexual emotions of a man. The other computer operators seemed to think of her as simply another piece of computer hardware. Since she worked three months at a time on the night shift and slept during the day, there was little time to meet any other men besides these computer sex-crazed maniacs. I had inadvertently reminded her once again of how boring and mechanical her life had become. Never mind about Andrea, she smiled to herself. However, outwardly she did try to show some concern.

"Let's go over to the logistics computer." She stood up and headed for one of the screens at the back of the room.

"This will show us if she has left Expom, or if she is still here. You do realize that she does do a lot of the reservation leg work around here?" Legwork was an understatement I thought to myself about the play on words. I nodded as if I agreed with her and that we were truly talking about the same subject.

She sat down in front of the large screen and motioned me to take a seat near her. She entered several codes into the keyboard and a list of names appeared on the screen. The list was very detailed and although the screen was the largest in the room, the names still appeared to be too small for my liking. "This will only take a second." By the time she had finished her sentence, a small red dot appeared on the screen next to the name Andrea Daniel. The names disappeared off the screen followed by a large printout on Andrea. This time the print was larger and I could read clearly what she had done and where she had been in the past six months. The list was an entire almanac of countries, dates, and who's who of nobility. The last entry was this evening. She had left for The Congo. Apparently Bill had scared the poor woman away for good.

"The flight just left a couple of hours ago. I could signal Flagstaff to have her call you if you would like?"

"No, that won't be necessary."

"Is there anything I could do for you?" She enthusiastically asked.

I gave her a devilish smile and said,

"Why yes there is. Would you like to join me for dinner tomorrow night?"

"Sorry, but I can't. I'm working fourteen hour shifts for the next couple of nights."

"When would be a good time?"

"In about three weeks, then I'll be off for a month." She solemnly stated.

"Are you going anywhere special?"

"No, I haven't made any plans yet."

"Have you ever been on a tropical island in the middle of the Pacific Ocean?"

"No, I haven't, but it does sound venturous." This was a word used by the so-called trendy people, but at times it seemed to slip into everyone's vocabulary.

"Splendid, I'll point out my name and address on your screen. All you have to do is tell me when you think you might like to come and I'll take care of the rest."

After talking a little while longer about the research island in Fiji and about what a great time she would have, I suddenly realized that I was taking up all of her working time. I quickly decided that I had better leave. After all, I had only just given her the confidence and trust to come to M.B.I.'s research island, and I didn't want to upset things by jeopardizing her job performance.

I raised out of my seat and was about to say good-bye, when I noticed that the screen had switched on to a new topic and little flashes of light now moved slowly across a three dimensional grid that resembled the topography of the moon. The image stopped me dead in my tracks.

"What is that?" I asked in a tone more professionally demanding than one out of curiosity. Upon hearing the authoritarian tone of voice, Julie immediately responded.

"This diagram shows where each person is that has left the confines of Expom." By the time she had finished blurting out the sentence, she had calmed down to normal. I at once recognized what I had done.

"Sorry, I didn't mean to make you jump, but could you please tell me how it works." This time my voice was an overwhelming tide of pleasantry. Inside I wondered how regimented the workers of Expom really were?

"Each moon suit has a built in transmitter that is in direct link with us."

"Is there a way to disarm the transmitter?"

"No, it's automatically activated when air flows and pressurizes the touring suits. If it fails to work properly or it senses an irregularity in air flow the entire suit is removed from usage until the situation has been corrected, but why would anyone want to tamper with it anyway?"

"No real reason," I began. "Just a thought nothing more. One other question though, does the range of the transmitter cover the entire surface of the moon?"

"Oh no," she smiled and said. "The transmitter is only good for about thirty Earth miles, but none of the activities are ever scheduled for more than twenty miles away from Expom."

She then paused for a moment while she thought. "Except for the moon cave," she continued.

"I thought that the moon cave was only five miles from here?"

"Oh, it's even closer than that, but there are a few places like inside the tunnel system where we can't pick up a thing on the screen. Dr. Slatski, the head of our Geological Survey Team, says that it's due to the meteorite composition of the region, and that there is nothing we can do about it. So from time to time when people are walking in the tunnels, we loose them on the screen, only to have them reappear moments later. We had to calibrate our computers to allow for the moon cave area, so that the alarms wouldn't be triggered every time someone exited or entered that area."

"That's very interesting," I smiled and said. "It must make your job more difficult though."

"I'm used to it," she responded.

"Tell me something, is there some place that Dr. Slatski usually visits near that area?"

"Why yes, the only reason I know, is because he is one of the few people that ever goes out alone, and when he does, he usually heads for one area that he is working at on the east side of the moon cave."

"Is this area one of the areas not detected by the transmitter?"

"Right in the heart of the mess. Maybe that's why he likes it there so much." I gave her an uncomprehending expression. "In case you haven't noticed," she continued. "We all think that he's slightly off his rocker. He stays away from the rest of us, and when someone does approach him, he seems as if he can't handle interpersonal situations. It's like he doesn't have any human social skills."

"Well, thanks for all the information, but I don't want to keep you any longer from your work."

"That's all right, I'm sure the work is still waiting for me."

"Nevertheless, I will be looking forward to your visit, and I shall see you soon."

Julie on the spur of the moment, jumped out of her chair and gave me a very passionate kiss. It surprised me at first, especially at work and all, but times have changed and the place did look deserted.

While she released her arms from around my neck, I tried to imagine what the month ahead with her would be like.

"Good-bye for now," I whispered as I turned to leave. I walked downstairs quietly until I reached the counter where Erik had his back turned, he quickly slipped by and disappeared down the dim lit corridor like a mysterious dark shadow. Erik thought he had heard a noise down the hall, but by the time he had finished fiddling with his files, the noise had vanished.

Back in my room, I stripped down and climbed into bed. I think I'll apply for a job here; I drowsily contemplated as I began to fall asleep. In my dreams that night, heaven had the form of Expom, and I was one of the lucky souls to pass by Peter's gates.

PAGE 157

The next morning, the alarm clock seemed to go off earlier than I expected. I double-checked with my own watch sitting on the nightstand before I realized that the clock was accurate, and it was time to wake up. Although getting out of bed proved to be another matter. My head was pounding and my stomach was growling. Then it dawned on me, that through all the activities last night, I still never had a chance to eat anything, and now I was famished. I sat on the edge of the bed and waited a minute for my head to clear. That will teach you to drink on an empty stomach, I said to myself. After taking a cold shower to bring myself back to reality, I proceeded to get dressed. I enjoyed cold showers, so this was no great sacrifice. From my early years as a young marine biologist, I had spent most of my time in one cold ocean or another, and now taking a cold shower reminded me of those earlier exploits and the carefree days of life. In fact, the only time that I could remember taking a hot shower had been while skiing in Aspen, Colorado. My hands at that time had turned so blue from the constant falls in the deep snow, which afterwards made a hot shower seem like a gift from the gods. Needless to say, I gave up the thrill of skiing and headed back to the Philippines where swimming with poisonous sea snakes seemed less hazardous than risking hypothermia. Since that time when my friends would suggest going back up to the slopes, I would just look at them and say, "You know, if you want to glide down a slope and stay warm at the same time, try body surfing in the south pacific. It's a lot cheaper and not a half hidden tree stump in sight." With this statement said the subject of skiing was usually dropped.

After getting dressed in a blue and gray jogging suit, I made my way to one of the many snack shops. I quickly ate an egg and teriyaki hamburger sandwich and drank a large cup of Irish cream flavored coffee. The smell of the coffee refreshed my senses and the caffeine was the final ingredient that I needed to psychologically get the day started. I hit the halls heading for the locker rooms, full well knowing that if Dean and Garret were going to show up for the tour, I had better first check to see if they had planted any of their practical jokes amongst my gear. As I made his way down the corridors, a familiar figure approached in my direction. It was none other than Dr. Slatski, but there was something odd in the way he carried himself. His face was very pale with his eyes slightly dilated, and his breathing was shallow and deliberate. I could not help but show immediate concern for the poor man.

"Dr. Slatski, is something wrong?" The doctor until now, had not noticed me coming his way, and the sound of a human voice jerked him back to awareness.

"I didn't mean to startle you, but are you alright?"

"Yes, I'm fine," he weakly replied. "I just need to catch my breath."

"Are you sure nothing is wrong." I was extremely skeptical at this point.

"Yes, I just over did myself on my morning walk. I'll be alright in a few minutes." I noticed that his rate of respiration had diminished, but still it seemed a little abnormal. "Please don't concern yourself over me. Honestly, I'll be fine."

"Alright, but I'll stop by and see how you are doing later." I said this half out of concern, and half because I wanted to discuss the aliens further.

"If you insist," Dr. Slatski replied as he began to walk past me. I waited for him to walk out of sight, before I resumed heading towards my destination. I knew that Dr. Slatski was ill, but I did not have a clue as to what his malady might be. Perhaps it was some form of lung disease, but since the doctor did not want to discuss it, I would drop it for now.

In the locker room there was a fresh group of people waiting anxiously to don their first moon suit. A few days before, I had been one of those starry eyed tourists; today, however, I had the appearance of a seasoned veteran. It showed not only in my eyes, but by the way I moved and handled my exposure suit. Within minutes I had my gear on, and was helping some of the newcomers with theirs. The tour guides recognized me from previous excursions and thanked me for my much-appreciated help. For the tour guides, any help with the tourists was welcomed with no questions asked. Especially if it was close to the end of the month, for a new crew would be taking over soon. The job was not that difficult, it's just that tourists can grate on one's nerves with such relentless speed. Over worked Earthlings saved for this one of a kind vacation for quite some time, and they were going to enjoy themselves, even if it meant making everyone around them miserable. So one had to act just as much a referee as tour guide when these strange migratory creatures congregated at Expom.

The tour was almost ready to begin. They had all suited up and had their helmets on. After a moment of pause while the head tour guide gave us a short speech on safety, we were all corralled over by the doors that lead to the moonrail. As I waited in line to board the shuttle bus, I grabbed the arm of the head tour guide and pulled him aside.

"I won't be going into the cave with you. I'm working with Bill Nico from the government, and that's all I can tell you. So don't panic when you see me go in the opposite direction of the moon cave." The man stood for a moment with a blank expression as he tried to recall the meeting the other day when an agent with the same last name of Nico, had asked a group of them several seemingly meaningless questions.

However, he did not want to get into any trouble so he quickly spoke up.

"Ok, whatever you want to do is fine with me."

I wasn't sure if this simple ploy would work, but from the sound of the answer, I smiled and congratulated myself. I could have gone through the proper channels of course but that would have bored me to tears. I would have nothing to do with anything that resembled governmental protocols and limitless supplies of red tape.

The tour guide released himself from my grasp and returned to helping board those passengers that were either failing in years or lacking exercise; two completely separate but indistinguishable categories at times. Soon the bus was heading; down the moonrail track and the tour guides had a brief moment to rest before the worst of their expectations would soon be realized.

Would the first of the group run down the tunnels and drag the rest of the group along? Would the first of the group move too slowly and bottle everyone up in the tunnels? Would they ask the most stupid question ever heard? Or would something greater in magnitude happen? These were only some of the questions that most likely ran through their minds. Yet if any should ask, they would quickly say that they loved their job and enjoyed the people that they met, for it was the overall pleasure of walking on the moon that solely counted.

When they arrived at the moonrail station, I waited for the tour to walk up the stairs towards the entrance of the cave, and then I began my walk to the east side of the great rocky slope. I knew the hike would be long, but by using the hopping-run method perfected by the early astronauts, it would take me less than ten minutes to reach the edge of the great wall which enveloped the entrance to the tunnels.

I covered the distance quickly, for my strides had improved considerably since my first attempt at walking on the moon. My movements had become more precise and the result of all this was that instead of being out of breath like one of the new tourists, I felt warm and ready to move on. I turned for a moment at the edge to view the landscape. The shuttle bus had left. Probably heading back to pick up another load of tourists. The area that minutes ago had been overrun by dozens of stumbling moon suits, now seemed lifeless, looking as if the area had been abandoned for centuries. Time seemed to stand still on the moon. Time was one of the most important things that man possessed, and without its presence, man felt naked without direction or purpose. Humans always surround themselves with pictures and objects that reminded them of things that had passed long ago in time or things that would come to be in time, but the thought of being surrounded in an environment such as the moon, without a sense of time was more than some could bare. Even I, who had spent half my life on tiny islands felt overwhelmed by the empty landscape.

"I wonder if man in the future will find it increasingly difficult to face these bleak surroundings as mankind populates more of the corners of the universe and the boundaries become even smaller," I asked the moonscape as if expecting some mysterious voice to echo back to me with an answer.

The edge of the wall lost its smooth perpendicular surface as it continued along its eastern most edges. The east cliff of the huge mountain was strewn with depressions created by impacting objects and their rubble littered the slope. It gave me the impression of a coral reef that had decayed centuries ago. With relief, I had found a point of reference for time.

"Here I am. What do I do now?" the words echoed inside my helmet. This side of the mountain seemed to stretch over a mile long and the first plateau was at least over a hundred feet high. Without a map, I couldn't even tell if there was more than one plateau or if this was the shortest side of the mountain. The thought of roaming over this barren domain was one of farthest thoughts in the back of my mind, but the thought of spying on or possibly encountering the aliens made it well worth the effort. So with a sigh of discontentment, I strolled halfway up the east face and began heading for the far side at a very slow pace.

This is fruitless, I said as I fumed to myself. I was standing at the other end of the ridge breathing heavily. Two hours had elapsed according to the red diodes implanted inside my helmet. Another two hours and I would have to start heading back towards the shuttle station. How could it be so difficult to find? The entrance would have to be large in order to move supplies in and out so relatively easy, or could it be that the entrance was concealed and it would once again be necessary to stomp one's feet until the ground beneath gave way? The top of the plateau yielded little more than a glimpse of a basin of rubble that formed the summit. Deep within the ground below me had to be strewn a great array of tunnels, with the aliens securely inhabiting somewhere inside them, far from the reach of the primitive beast, from which I descended, called man. To find the aliens would be one thing, but what to do next was still another matter. In a way, not being able to find them seemed to solve more problems than if I did find them. Would I have tried to talk with them or walk right in unannounced and say I am your friend, tell me something about yourselves? If the Indians of Brazil thought this a rude and brash method of introduction, what would an alien race think? There was always silent observation, but where would that get me? I did precisely that approach when they were stealing the cargo area. In the end, there was no real good solution, and I decided to play it by ear, but failing to find the entrance, seemed to nullify even this rudimentary plan. Discouraged and tired, I began to walk across the top of the plateau towards the moonrail station. Tomorrow I'll be back with the probe, I decided. If I had thought that finding the aliens was going to be so difficult, I would have used the deep-sea probe in the first place. After all, why did I do all that pointless running around and wasting all of my energy? Besides, the sheer weight of the probe alone might be my best bet for gaining entrance in to the tunnels. Nothing ever seemed to work out as easily as it did in the movies. If it were going to take more than just pure luck to meet these aliens, then I would just have to work out the solution. I kept all of this in mind as I made my way back, and with every step throwing up swirls of gray-white dust.

After a brief period of time had passed, I looked up from the ground and saw at the top of the stairs, the first group of tourists returning from the caves. I stood up, brushed off the back of his pants that had been resting on the moonrail, and moved over to the main area where the shuttle bus would meet them. Within minutes the rest of the tour group arrived and I saw shuttle bus in the distance making its way down the rail.

"Did you enjoy your private tour?" the head guide sarcastically asked me.

"Rather uneventful," I answered politely.

"I could have told you that," the guide said in a muffled voice. "Nothing out there except rubble."

"Is that why Dr. Slatski goes out there every day?" At this the guide seemed to flinch and the expression on his face changed dramatically. There was anger or maybe even a hint of fear in his eyes.

"Listen you," he bellowed out in a voice that cared not who heard or what those around might think. "He's not your normal scientist. The man is nuts, so anything that he does should be weighed with a grain of salt." He fell silent and walked away, not giving me a chance to question him further. Whatever I had done to make this man so angry would have to be left unanswered. I knew that the doctor did not behave altogether status quo, but this guide seemed to suggest something more significant by the usage of the word normal.

On the way back to Expom, the guide sat in the forward compartment and I sat in the aft. The tourists had made it impossible for me to squeeze my way forward before we left the shuttle station adjacent to the moon cave. Now all the front seats were occupied and I would have to wait until we docked at Expom before I could remove my hose from the main outlet connecting all the tourists to the main ventilation system. I had to admit one thing, granted that it kept me in my seat like a leash; the air inlet was very cool and refreshing. The ventilation system took away all of the foul odors that had accumulated, permeated, and saturated my suit during the course of my fruitless expedition. I started laughing to myself, if only the air system could do the same for the odor of Limburger cheese. It would be some time before I could look another Russian straight in the face and contain my humor.

The trip inbound to Expom seemed quicker than outbound. Time always seemed to slip away faster when you had something on your mind and it seemed to linger on endlessly when you were waiting for time to pass by; such a natural paradox, such a welcomed natural phenomenon when it was to your advantage. Soon I could see the doors that lead to the Expom moonrail station.

As we neared, the doors began to swing open and the familiar silver material glistened on the walls as it reflected the rays of the sun. This time however, I didn't wonder why the markings were there, but why they seemed to be so ubiquitous. Why should they have examined or spied on the activities of Expom so closely unless they had more in mind than simply repairing or re-supplying their ship and leaving in peace? Without more input, speculation on this point seemed futile.

The shuttle bus docked and the air filled tube ramps were connected to the various doors of the bus compartments. Within seconds I was standing in front of my assigned locker. I quickly undressed and placed my suit haphazardly in the locker. I slapped the locker door shut and went in search of the guide. The locker room was packed, but the section for the guides was set apart from those of the tourists, which made the chances of finding him easier. Sure enough, as I rounded the corner and headed down another corridor full of lockers, I saw the man walking with a towel around his waist heading for the showers. I walked down the corridor and turned yet another corner that led to the showers. There I saw the man standing in one of the stalls with a handful of shampoo in his hair. There was only one other person in the shower room that had a capacity for twelve total stalls, and this other young guy was deep in thought, eyes closed, with hot steamy recycled water pounding down on the back of his neck.

"I hate to bother you, but do you mind telling me what you meant about the doctor?" The guide stopped rubbing the suds into his hair and tried to say something, but inadvertently the soap got in his mouth and he had to spit out the loathsome material. He rinsed off the front of his face and looked at me in disgust. Meanwhile, the short young fat guy who first appeared asleep standing under the water, had opened his eyes at the sound of another voice, but nothing more.

"Look, the man is not like you or me. OK? I know it for a fact."

"Could you tell me why?"

"Why are you so interested?"

"Let's just say that we don't see eye to eye either."

"Ok, but Charles can tell you better." He nodded his head in the direction of the other man. The short young fat guy had an apprehensive look that filled his face.

"It's alright, tell him" the guide said to Charles.

"He wasn't like that when he first came here," Charles hesitantly began. "I've noticed the difference only over the past year or so."

"What kind of difference?"

"Not much at first, little things, the type that don't really mean much, but now I'm not so sure." His voice began to trail off.

"Tell him about this week," the guide spoke up. Charles was silent for a minute as he contemplated what to do, then he said, "Last week Dr. Slatski came back from one of his daily trips, but looking real sick. We didn't think much of it because we're always getting a lot of tourists sick while on tours. So we just thought it had finally caught up with him too, but when I went to fill up his air tanks, I found out the real reason. They were bone dry," he paused as if to give this very sovereign significance, then he continued. "You can't have empty tanks or else you're dead. Do you see what I mean?" I nodded in confirmation and Charles continued, now with a very hushed tone.

"I know we shouldn't have, but we wanted to see whether he was just lucky or if something was going on. You know, like if he had found gold nearby or something else that would give him a reason to lie about his long walks. Well, anyway, we fixed his tanks so that he would have only thirty minutes worth of air once away from the shuttle. Of course he had an emergency supply of air good for three hours, so it wasn't like we were trying to kill him or anything. The point is, he didn't return on the next shuttle like he should have under such circumstances. As a matter of fact, he was gone for over three hours, and he had never flicked his emergency supply on. We would have known about it immediately because when the emergency system is activated, Expom is automatically alerted and a rescue team is sent out to investigate. So where do you suppose he got that extra air and what is so important that it is worth risking his life for?"

"I couldn't begin to guess," I began. "But I think that the good doctor will tell me." The other two men looked at me with eyes widened. They would never have been so bold as to risk their jobs in order to ask such a private question of a senior staff member, but this man was going to and they were not sure as to how this would effect their positions on Expom. I could see their concern and quickly spoke up. "I can assure you that no mention of your names will be made. This is strictly a personal matter between the doctor and myself." I thanked the two men and walked away.

"Do you think we should have trusted him?" Charles said as soon as he was sure that I had left the locker room.

"There is no one that we can trust, but I think that we at least have a fifty-fifty chance with him."

"You really know how to reassure a person!"

"Yeah, that's why I'm the boss and you are my assistant."

Having been armed with this new information, I decided to once again have another chat with Dr. Slatski. This time however, I was certain that I would obtain all the information that I desired. As crazy as my idea might be, I still was convinced that I knew why the good doctor behaved the way he had and also why time was so important. I came to the conclusion that the more time that elapsed; the more difficult it would be to keep the unfolding situation under control. I couldn't shake this feeling as I made my way towards the good doctor's office.

PAGE 172

As I approached the door to the science center, I could clearly see Dr. Slatski sitting at his desk busily striking his fingers on a wireless keyboard. As the door slid open, the doctor pressed one of the buttons on the panel box situated on the left side of his desk. The computer screen quickly lowered itself into the desktop. Halfway down, the screen swiveled from a vertical position to horizontal, and came to a stop as it became flush with the top of the desk. He placed his folded hands on the desk and in great frustration looked up at me.

I think that it's time we had another little chat Dr. Slatski or whoever you are." I challenged him before any form of greeting could be made. No doubt the doctor had been on guard the moment he saw me, but I don't think he ever expected my bold accusation, and the expression on his face expressed his shock, but only for a fraction of a second. He was speechless. He was exposed, and he had no idea as to how he could continue to maintain control of the current situation.

"I realize that this might have come as a shock to you, but don't worry." I said with a smug look on my face. "In fact, I'll even help you out of this jam, that is, if you answer a few questions and I find the answers satisfactory."

The doctor leaned back in his chair, folded his arms across his chest, looked up at the ceiling, and began to ponder the situation. As Dr. Slatski concentrated, I decided to settle into a chair on the opposite side of the desk and make myself comfortable. I could relax now; after all, time was on my side and against the doctor.

The doctor found the situation almost unbearable. There in front of him sat a man relishing his position, knowing that within minutes he could destroy years of planning and ruin all chances of the marooned crew to ever reach their homeland. He scrutinized me one final time and demanded, "How do I know I can trust you?"

"You don't, but then again, you have no choice. Your plans, whatever they are, will not succeed and you and your alien race will be exposed to the rest of the world. I'm not exactly sure why that is such a great threat to you, but I'm willing to bet on it anyway. It may put you at ease though, if you knew of my intentions. As a scientist, I must know about you and your race, and since you have not shown any prior ill intentions towards my species, I feel the need to reciprocate in like kindness. Do we understand one another?"

"Agreed, but this will be for you and you alone."

"Agreed." I leaned forward in the chair with my elbows planted on my knees, and waited expectantly.

"First of all, out of curiosity, when did you first become aware of me?" Some of the tension seemed to leave his body and he looked a little more at ease.

"From the moment we first shook hands. Your grip felt unnatural. My hand tingled for several minutes afterwards. Just like after touching the silver substance. I found that to be a strange coincidence."

"I see," he murmured. "Well, I'll start you off with some background before info first." Dr. Slatski was the first to hear our story, he found it hard to follow, but then that was before we realized that you had to have all sentences in a specific order of sequence before you could interpret the whole of the subject matter: our mistake; and very trying for the doctor. But then I will return to what happened to him in due time." He paused, took a deep breath and continued. "To begin with, we illegally entered into the restricted zone that bordered closely around Earth."

"Why was Earth restricted?" I interrupted.

"I'll answer that in due time as well. But to make my story clearer, I had better make you aware about my race and some history before I go into our adventure into restricted Earth space. Our planet was populated over ten million years ago. Since that time we have changed very little. We look the same today as we did then; only our customs and social values have improved. When our forefathers first descended to my world from the heavens, they found simple celled organisms and plants representing the only native life forms. Nothing else is known about them, except for the early period of time when they were trying to cultivate their civilization, eventually, wars beyond your comprehension engulfed the planet and left the survivors weary of the future and ill in thought, or should I say in contempt for the past. All records were lost and now the only thing we can remember is that we did not evolve on our planet and because of this, there must be others like us hidden somewhere by the vastness of space. One other quick point, we had no God or Gods. I guess that this was actually a blessing in disguise, for it would have only fractured our people even more, as it has done on Earth with your pointless Holy wars."

"You might have a point there," I agreed. "But a lot of us still feel a need for a God anyway."

"So you do. That's not really my concern, but to continue with my story, because of our past, there were many unanswered questions? So we tried to find a civilization in hope of finding out what we are and where we came from. After five million years had passed, we found a planet similar to ours where life existed. That planet had a rich fossil history and an on going chain of evolution. That particular planet was Earth." He stopped for a brief moment as if waiting for me to comment, and then he proceeded. "When we arrived on Earth, it was at the dawn of hominids. We observed them carefully for they were un-precedently similar to ourselves. There was even speculation by some scientific communities as to how these creatures would evolve and possibly resemble us or at least gain the ability to think like us.

"It was at this point in time when things began to change. Within a hundred years, which is rather a small period of time for genetic evolution, a couple of species of early hominid predecessors began to evolve. Not at a normal rate and remarkably similar to a primitive likeness of ourselves. There had been no environmental change to induce such an event, so a team was sent in to investigate. Soon an independent report was filed that suspected genetic tampering by a group of scientists too eager to let natural selection take its own natural course. The scientists in question eventually admitted their guilt of tampering and resigned from the scientific community, but irreparable damage had already been done and the species whose genes that they spliced with our own, no less, had become well established on Earth." Having said this much he stood up and walked over to the book shelves covering the wall. He stared at the titles of the books as if seeming to read them, but his gaze was retrospective. After a few silent moments he began to pace with small quick strides and looked in my direction.

"You know that even in modern humans, 98% of your DNA is the same as that in Chimpanzees, so it doesn't take much of a change to make a new species. That's why in order to safeguard Earth from further genetic contamination or alteration, certain rules and biological protocols were enacted. Permits were required to venture even close to Earth and no one, I believe, was ever allowed to land. Of course, there was still an occasional emergency situation that was unavoidable considering crash landings due to power failure and so forth.

Then about 45 thousand years ago in Europe, there was another large disposition of one species and the takeover by a new one that seemed to have arisen quite unexpectedly. With the question of tampering materializing once again, those in power became furious and new measurements were taken to safeguard Earth. One measure taken was the installation of the black box, which is a navigational device that is linked to our onboard computers. If for any reason a ship with one of these devices installed accidentally enters Earth's restricted zone, the device will detonate and our core reactors will destroy the ship. The ship would literally disintegrate with all hands on board; even if there were any survivors, they would be dealt with most aggressively."

"Now having been given a brief outline of our background, I believe that you will be able to understand the following more clearly." He stopped pacing, cleared his throat, and hesitated a little longer while I sat patiently enthralled, waiting for the story to continue. "You now know that it was my people's great curiosity that first lead us to your planet, it was also curiosity that made us tamper with the black box so that we could see for ourselves what was taking place with your culture. We knew that we were risking our lives, but that was a chance that we decided to take. So after entering the restricted zone and finding that our tampering had been successful, we wanted to first investigate what you had accomplished here on the moon. This allowed us to cautiously explore without immediate detection by those on Earth or by those from our own world. It also lessened our degree of anxiety. We began to circle the moon in order to find our first point of interest. We were already aware of your early lunar landing craft, and our own scientists had relayed this information to us. So we were looking for something a little more recent, something that we could discover and investigate on our own. That's when we came across an object not far from this very spot. We had never seen anything quite like it before, so it was a must that we drop our speculations and find out just exactly what we had found. So from word of my former commander, we sent out a team to investigate the object."

"I believe I already know what happened next," I interjected. "It was a military device." Upon hearing these words the alien cringed, then lowered his head and whispered, "We lost half the crew on board when that device exploded. It was as if it had collapsed our very ship." He strode over to his desk and resumed pacing behind it, keeping his gaze directed at me as he relived the incident. It was as clear to him now as the day it had transpired. "I was knocked unconscious. A member of my crew woke me up. I was immediately informed that the captain had been killed and that I was now in charge. You know what I did? I began to laugh. Captain of what? That was all I could think. Needless to say, I wasn't very rational at the time. So my crew waited, and while they waited, those that were injured over time gave up hope." He stopped his pacing and sat down behind the desk, like a weary soldier just fresh from the battlefront. His shoulders slumped down, his face suddenly looking old and haggard. I leaned back into the chair and quietly tried to visualize the scene.

"When I had returned to my senses, and the pounding in my head quit interfering with my thoughts, we came to the conclusion that the only way we would ever leave the moon and return home, would be with the aid and resources of Earth. So we hid everything underground and patiently waited. By that point, there were some fifty of us left alive. We had enough chambers intact to keep thirty-five of us in suspended animation until necessary. This left fifteen of us to subsist anyway we could until help arrived. That period of time seemed to linger on endlessly. By the time your people arrived to build Expom, only nine of the original fifteen were left to greet you, but we dared not. We needed your help, but could not risk your personal intervention.

The short-term solution was to borrow what we needed to survive. At one stage we even contemplated commandeering one of your space shuttles in hopes of landing at some desolate site on Earth, where we could not have been found, but still exist.

"What stopped you?"

"We encountered the real Dr. Slatski. He noticed our tracks, and one day followed one of the crewmembers back to our ship, or what was left of it. When he first walked into our camp, we were horrified. He came marching in as if he had been there many times and as if he owned the place. He wore a big cheerful smile, and his arms were outstretched in a gesture of friendship. The whole incident was overwhelming, and with no room for debate, he was accepted. After all, as then as it is now, we had nothing to loose. Our supplies were dwindling fast, with no real solutions in sight. We were very desperate."

"Then what happened to him?" I asked.

"Dr. Slatski was a great man," he continued. "I have yet to find many among you like him. We shared between us things that are normally kept to ourselves. We had a bond that did not differentiate between our races, but was strictly founded on the similarities of our thoughts and ideas. We were as close as brothers from the same womb. That is why when his heart failed him; I also felt the sudden pain. It's not a normal custom in my race to form such deep bonds except with close relatives, so the whole experience was very traumatic. I had no idea how genetically flawed you humans are. Trying to save him proved futile, even with the advanced equipment that we have at our disposal."

"I'm sorry," I solemnly replied.

"That time has passed. However, prior to his death, we had formulated a plan to build another ship that would take us home. The plan called for the utilization of materials from Earth by redirecting the necessary cargo to Expom, and then simply removing it from the warehouses before the cargo was returned to its original destination. Because we ran the entire operation by computer, we hoped that the lost cargo would become permanently lost in paperwork or filed away forever in some data bank. However, we either underestimated your government, or Dr. Slatski had been too enthusiastic about the timing of our completion. We have also run into several unforeseen complications. To solve the most critical problems facing us, I became Dr. Slatski and continued on in his place. This way I was able to personally supervise the ordering of parts, and take care of any other unforeseen circumstances."

"You are aware, of course, of the investigation being conducted this very minute by the government," I said.

"I believe you are referring to Bill Nico," he stated matter-of-factly. I was not surprised by this response. I merely was curious as to how this alien was going to complete his mission with this new complication.

"You see we are very close to the completion of our ship. With the arrival of the next shipment from Earth we will soon be ready to leave the moon. Now, it seems that the final stage of our endeavor will rest on your shoulders as well as ours. So you must ask yourself if you should help us. Don't misunderstand me, not always have those that were found to have violated the restricted zone been eliminated immediately, for there have been a few crash landings and things of that nature, but with us, our purpose was strictly against the rules and if we are caught, I see little leniency for our crime. You see, in their eyes Earth is nothing more than an experiment, and we have uncorked the bottle, contaminated the growing culture, and deliberately ruined the experiment. Such an action cannot be passively shrugged aside. So I ask you once again, what do you plan to do? Our fate may well rest in your hands."

"Don't ask me to play God with your lives," I said. My voice was stern and heavy. I looked directly into the clear hazel-blue eyes of the alien as if to read his thoughts. This is a very dangerous entity, I thought. I must be very careful. These creatures are desperate, and desperation causes unpredictable reactions. For all I know he killed Dr. Slatski and took his place to speed up the necessary supply shipments. They are very close to lift off, and I could ruin years and years of planning by simply telling Bill, which of course he must already realize, but by eliminating me too soon and causing even more suspicion and they might not get that last shipment. I tore my gaze away from his hypnotizing eyes and walked over to the large-scale moon model hanging from the ceiling. While staring at it I tried to imagine surviving in tunnels underneath the dull gray-white surface with little hope of rescue. As I lifted his fingers to touch the rough surface, I directed my voice to the alien. "As a humanitarian, it is my duty to help, but it's your own wrong doing that put you in this situation. So any consequences should rest ill at ease with you and you alone. I don't relish the idea that you see us as a pet project imprisoned in a glass jar, but I feel that we are basically similar, and maybe someday when you see us eye to eye, our two races may become allies. In fact, using our terrible problem with curiosity as a cross cultural comparison, your tampering with our genetic pool has made us more alike than your race would presently like to think."

"I would have to agree with you." The alien watched me closely as he studied the moon model. "But it's unfortunate that the rest of my kind do not share my views of friendship, and that is where the issue stands. Still, I see that we are not the only ones that are prejudice. We see you Earthlings as all the same, one giant mass of primitive primates, yet you still pathetically distinguish traits among yourselves, which proves that neither of our races have yet achieved total perfection."

"I too will agree with that. Now what is it that you would have me do?"

"The first thing that you can do, is to persuade Mr. Nico to give approval and re-confirm the shipment of electronic equipment that was scheduled to arrive here two days from now. I believe that you are already familiar with the list of items."

"You don't need my help with that! I've already done that for you."

"You may have thought you had, but last night I believe Mr. Nico had second thoughts. The cancellation request was fed into the system sometime early this morning, and I've been trying for the last seven hours to change them." I sighed. I had no idea how I could be persuasive with no leverage to work with, but I would at least try.

"I'll have another word with him. The shipment will be here in two days as scheduled. Nevertheless, I would like to see your progress so far."

"Very well then, I shall meet you at the locker room on C deck tomorrow morning at nine. I have some classes to attend to this afternoon and an informal lecture this evening. I should attend, after all I don't need anymore suspicion cast on my shadow than I already have. I would like you to attend the if at all possible. The subject is on various phenomenon including black holes, and even though you may not enjoy astronomy, I'm sure that you'll at least find my speculations very intriguing."

"Hmm, I'll be looking forward to it, until then I'll try to find Bill and get things straightened out."

I extended my hand, not intending to shake hands with the doctor, but merely as a reminder as to how the doctor had first betrayed himself. The gesture was understood, and a slight grin appeared on the alien's face. He shook my hand and once again my hand tingled. I turned and left the room.

The alien, alias Dr. Slatski, stretched out his arms, inhaled and exhaled a deep breath, and for the first time in several critical weeks, set everything aside, satisfied that everything was running along smoothly. A thrill of anticipation ran up his spine at the thought of actually leaving the moon. However this feeling did not last long; new thoughts with new problems funneled into his brain. Thoughts that were taxing and once again he found himself futilely trying to escape them. There was no way to resolve them now. He remembered the first time he had met the human, Dr. Slatski, and a shaft of agony went through him. His thoughts returned once again to the present; tests needed to be performed, but in the end he knew he would have to put his theories in action, and in doing so, risk his life along with the lives of his entire crew; not something that even in his culture, would be dealt with lightly, especially in view of other recent catastrophic events. There really wasn't any other choice for him right now, not that he was a believer in religions, but fates are fates, and any and all fates are impossible to predict or control, but given time, at the right moment, fates could be altered.

PAGE 186

    I walked down the long corridor towards Bill's room. I didn't expect to find him there, but I had few other places to search. In fact, I wouldn't have been surprised to find him outside Expom, searching in vain for the aliens. So much for them, I chuckled. They were so close to humans genetically, that for all intense purposes, humans could be classified as one of their sub-species. I wondered what alterations actually had to be performed to make the alien resemble the exact facial features of Dr. Slatski? Maybe to them plastic surgery was considered simple and an ordinary procedure. There wasn't anyway for me to calculate the total extent of their technological abilities until I could at least get a glimpse of their damaged ship. Tomorrow this would be my prime objective.

    As I stood in front of the door to Bill's room, I pressed a button on the side of the door and a heat sensitive tuning device was activated. I could hear the lightly ringing chimes emanating from behind the door. The signal ended and silence once again ensued. What now? I wondered, looking around and seeing no one, I coughed and cleared my throat.

    "Bill Nico" I said in a low voice. Nothing happened. My voice sounded roughly the same, but I had put too much emphasis on low pitch and not enough on the nasal resonance, so I tried once again. This time my voice improved. The door opened, I quickly passed through as I reflected back to when I was working on my graduate degree. All those empty hours of recording data and mimicking the birds and seals for self-entertainment had finally paid off. I could still imitate every wretched, fish-smelling seal that lived on that tiny island, where I had spent an entire summer. What had surprised me the most was the humanistic behavioral characteristics that accompanied their barks and grunts. The longer I stayed on the island, the more human like their behaviors seemed to become. I could still remember dreaming of conversations with them months after I had left the island. This was one of the few times in the past years where these memories had been evoked. They were still as vivid as the day they happened. Funny, I thought, how you could remember a time so lonely and long ago and find it difficult to remember a lively conversation that had taken place only months ago or a few days ago. And why did I think of that particular time rather than some more pleasant time instead?

The memories lasted only for a few moments; I was now standing in the center of the room, carefully looking for clues to the whereabouts of Bill. All appeared to be in order. Bill must have been in the military a long time I mused. The room was just too tidy for any other explanation. Not even a pair of socks lingered out of place in one of the corners. Socks out of place had always been one of my hotel trademarks. Bill is definitely too neat I decided. It was then that I noticed the computer was still on with something displayed on the screen. I walked over to it and peered closely at the contents. It was a list of cargo. The list was identical to the one I had seen in Dr. Slatski's office. The list remained on the screen for over a minute, and then it was replaced by a set of instructions. The instructions quickly left the screen and the cargo list reappeared. It was obvious what was going on. Bill had set up a program in order to find out who was the inside man for the cargo thefts. The screen changed back and forth several times while I patiently watched. Dr. Slatski was getting closer to the correct code, for his commands seemed to stay on the screen longer each time before being rejected. Then while I took a quick glance around the room, a beeping noise began to ding and my attention was once again focused on the computer screen. Across it read: shipment to arrive Thursday. Approval verified. Security code 0001624476abza. Science Reference Center, Dr. Slatski key user. So all Bill had to do now was read this and he could end his search. I wonder how the activities of Dr. Slatski had gone undetected until now? Now, how to change this, I wondered. He placed his hands on the keyboard when suddenly the door opened and a voice shouted out, "Don't touch one thing." It was stern and demanding and I felt compelled to obey. I turned to face the door and was met by the gaze of Bill. He appeared unsettled, but a quick look at the screen changed his entire mood. "So it's him is it? I thought it might be," he gleefully stated.

"What do you plan to do?"

"Nothing, absolutely nothing," Bill said with a big grin.

"I only did it to find out who was behind all this, I had no intention of actually stopping the shipment. I only wanted to find out where they are going to take it. Chances are I'll then be able to recover all the past shipments; all at the same time, and as for the aliens or whoever they are, I'll deal with them later."

"I guess all this makes you a double agent Dr. Wilson!" Bill laughed. I was surprised by the accusation. "I realize that you didn't plan it, but I've been with the service a long time, and I know the symptoms of the Stockholm effect quite well. Of course this isn't the standard scenario, but whether I deal with Russians, aliens, or whoever, U.S. policy comes first. I think that you had better remember that too. Although being a scientist, you might find it difficult to face the real world and accept my ideas."

"Don't get your personal prejudices entwined with reality." I said. "I realize the job you have to do, but at the same time I would rather use reason to sort out this situation as opposed to your method of an unrelenting show of force. There is a lot more at stake here than missing cargo, and I would like you to be aware of that fact."

"One thing at a time, and we will do it my way." Bill commanded. I stood silent. Bill took this as a nonverbal consent. He was sure that I could still be useful and that events had turned in his favor. I was increasingly finding this man to be a disgusting creature. I was sure that given enough time, this man could even make the Russians look good. It was obviously inherent in his personality.

"Now then, I need to find out from you where they are hiding the cargo?" I smiled and looked at him for a moment. I was beginning to find this situation comical.

"I realize that this is going to sound like a worn out expression, but I don't have any idea. I went out looking for their so-called hideout, but I found absolutely nothing. Maybe you can do better, but I doubt it. They have it well hidden, and the only way you are going to find them is by a guided tour. Preferably one given by Dr. Slatski himself, so you won't be risking your life or even worse, get lost."

"I think I could convince him." Bill stated menacingly.

"As a matter of fact I already have." Bill's eyes widened a bit and I sensed that this was as much emotion as this man could portray at any one time. "I'm going to one of his lectures this evening, and then first thing in the morning he is going to take me there. Would you like to come along?"

"No thanks. That is, I would like to attend the lecture, but I think I'll pass on the tour." This surprised me and yet peaked my curiosity. Why would he be so contradictory unless there was more to it than I could discern at this point.

"It may sound odd, but I don't have any choice. I will meet with him later on. Also, I don't want you to mention the fact that we even spoke with one another. Is that understood?" His voice sounded more militaristic and uncompromising with each word.

"Ok, I don't get it, but have it your way," I relented. Is he out to lunch or are all government agents like this? The question would have to remain open for the present time; I hoped he knew what he was doing.

PAGE 192

Time had eluded me and before I knew it, it was after three pm. I was receiving internal signals reminding me that I had completely forgotten about lunch, and for that matter breakfast too. Now my primary thought after ending the estranged meeting with Bill was to find food. Fast foods preferably: for I am an American, and fast food and Americans were synonymous, or at least inseparable.

Around the corner I found what I was looking for, a quick sandwich deli. Wolfing down a thick crusted multi-meat triple-decker and a cool beer did the trick to revive my flagging energy. Afterwards, there were still over four hours to kill before the lecture would begin. With this amount of time, I calculated that I could easily fit in a quick trip to the planetarium, located near the lecture hall. I had been in several planetariums on Earth, including those in the northern hemisphere that specialized in the northern stars, and also the southern hemisphere planetariums such as in Australia, where they concentrated on the Southern Cross and other related star clusters. Only in the southern hemisphere, they accented the names of various clusters of stars in unusual ways. In all, I had a relatively good idea about the heavens, but I still enjoyed watching as the machines turned, pivoted and made the entire sky change from one season to the next in a matter of seconds. This planetarium was very special, and had features that separated it from all the rest. For one thing, the dome was transparent, but unlike most clear surfaces, it magnified the view by a factor of a thousand. This meant that stars far away could appear only meters away on the other side of the dome. It was a major feat to produce such a visual spectacle, and in my opinion, it was well worth the effort, for the view was spectacular.

I entered the planetarium just in time for the next show. I barely had time to sit and view the natural stars before several plates raised out of their recessed storage positions, on the outside of the dome, and began to block my view. When the plates finally met at the top, and the room had become dark, the show began. Same old format, I thought disappointedly. It then dawned on me that no matter how much you spend on trying to make the heavens look real, they still looked like a bunch of boring little led lights. Of course I was sure that there were a couple of astronomy students in the crowd that would have vigorously disagreed with me. There were, however, a couple of segments such as the Milky Way galaxy that even I had to agree were worth the entire show. So in the end I felt that my time had been well spent, and I decided to stay behind, after most of the other tourists had left. Soon the plates that had covered the dome unlocked from one another and began descending back into their original recessed positions. Simultaneously the stars gradually sent their light into the dimly lit room. I thought that this change was as entertaining as the main show itself. Yet only a few stayed behind long enough to enjoy the view.

"Dr. Slatski will be giving a presentation in the adjacent room." A thin young man wearing an Expom company shirt came in and announced." From what I read on an electronic bulletin board the presentation wouldn't be too technical, and would be basically aimed at tourists with a limited knowledge of geology and astronomy. The announcer departed as abruptly as he entered. The few of us remaining, shuffled into the adjacent room where we saw others filling in from the opposite side entrance.

The room that it was held in was similar to the old rooms that I had spent a great deal of time in during my former years of college. It was large, slanting uphill toward the back end, with a small blackboard on the wall at the front end. Dr. Slatski stood in the front part of the room next to a slide projector waiting to begin the lecture. The time was 7:28. The presentation was supposed to start at 7:30. As soon as the two languid minutes past by, Dr. Slatski began what was the beginning of a very long oration. I found the lecture over simplified and I was daydreaming sooner than I expected. I tried my best to figure out what the doctor had wanted me to get out of his narration, but it took all my effort just to stay awake. It was a waste of time I thought to have such a man, or alien as the case may be, orating on subjects so simple, when the knowledge that he kept hidden inside his mind could be used to revolutionize the world overnight, but then again that was another matter. The session proceeded for twenty-five minutes or more. Dr. Slatski had time to give each person in the room several quick glances; that extra personal touch that humans so duly required. By doing so, he was able to spot me in the crowd. He needed to know where I was to make sure when the time came; I would be attentive and listen closely to what he had to say. Sure enough, when it was time, he noticed the far away look in my eyes, and the slight slumping of my body in the chair. He thought this might happen, and he had been right. The only people who ever kept close attention were tourists that had little previous knowledge of space. With the set format he was required to follow, the rest would just have to be patient from time to time.

"Dr. Wilson, you might find this interesting," he stated as he looked directly at me. I immediately became alert. I expected the cue to be subtler, but since my arrival at Expom, what I expected and what came to pass had been very different. Fortunately, the rest of the people sitting around me did not respond by turning towards me with gawking glances, which would have brought onto me an undue amount of embarrassment.

Dr. Slatski had been talking about black holes. His last statements that I could recall dealt with decreasing volume and increasing mass as an object plummeted closer to the center of a black hole. None of which was new to me.

"One of the theories surrounding the outer rings of a black hole." the doctor continued, "is that through such rings at a certain velocity, in order to avoid the attritional properties of the core itself, it may be possible to break the barriers of time. The ring or void that appears as a ring may actually be a doorway from one dimension to another. Now I realize that many of you maybe skeptical of this new theory, but you must keep in mind that most theories sound ridiculous until proven one way or another, and it's the realization of past theories that made it possible for you to visit Expom in the first place. So I hope you will all look at this with an open mind, and may be later on will contemplate the potential possibilities that are evoked. Now I'll leave you with that thought. If you would like to attend this presentation again or would like to have any questions answered, please feel free to come back here on Wednesday or stop by and visit any time that the science and information center is open. Thank you." Dr. Slatski stood and patiently waited for the tourists to file out of the room. As several of them approached, he pointed towards me. "Why don't you meet me in my office, and I'll answer your questions there." He rapidly turned without stopping to catch his breath to address one of the visitors.

"Yes, what can I do for you?"

I slowly rose to my feet while waiting for an opening in the crowd. I brushed by the mob surrounding the doctor, and in turn exited the room. I figured that it would be at least another fifteen minutes before the doctor could escape. With my usual style I decided that it was an excellent time to get something quick to snack on.

Having eaten, I nonchalantly made my way over to the center. The alien had not yet returned. Looking for something to do, I picked up a tablet off of a low setting coffee table, sat down and began to thumb through one of the online magazines. This is an odd magazine to have here, I pondered. The name of it was Four Wheeler, a relatively old publication, but one of the few auto magazines that persisted to endure the changing times. The basic format had changed little over the years. However, the machinery and technological advances had turned the magazine from its former simple country-boy gas power style, to one of high tech lithium battery and methane professionalism. With the world becoming increasingly smaller, more and more cutback publications were already well entrenched as urban or metropolitan online monthlies. Four Wheeler was no exception. At least the pictures are interesting I decided. Having lived on so many small islands it gave me a total lack of interest in electric cars; wind powered boats and solar powered 4 wheeler carts were by far more useful. Just then, the alien strode through the doorway.

"I see you found something to keep yourself amused. Sorry I'm late, but you know how some people can get carried away once you've sparked their interest."

"No problem, I expected as much." I quickly swiped my finger across the remaining pages while the doctor removed some papers from his briefcase. He then looked up at me.

"I couldn't help but notice how enthused you were over the lecture, but I am restricted as to how technical I can be."

"I can always use a good review on the basics, but what about this theory concerning the black holes? Have you already proved it?"

"Not exactly, but we have indications that it will work. You'll soon see that our project depends on this theory." I was really puzzled by this statement. "To build a ship and leave this desolate place is one thing, but to not know where to go next complicates everything. We can't just simply build a replica craft and speed back to our own world without them wondering what had happened to us for the last couple of decades. As you can imagine, they would eventually find out, and we would all be sentenced to death. Since none of us are looking forward to that consequence, I have come up with two others alternative plans. One, we could search for our very own small planet that we could colonize ourselves. This plan is the safest, but there is no telling how long it would take to find such a home, or if we ever could. Also, most of us have already passed our breeding stage, so the populating of such a planet would progress too slowly for those of us left to benefit from the results. Meaning that we have all gone through too much to lay the foundation on a world for a generation other than ourselves. This, therefore, leads us to our second plan, that although risky, promises a better life as the end result. That is why I wanted you to listen to the lecture. I don't want you to think that we are mad, but we are going to sacrifice our ship along with our lives to test the theory."

"You mean like you tested your theory and played with the R.E.D.S device? The one that nearly blew up in your face?" I sarcastically added.

"Yes, but this is entirely different. You see if we can break through the void and go back in time, there is a possibility that we can return home at an earlier date where our arrival would not be held with such suspicion."

"That is of course if you can plan the timing of your arrival."

"We have a theory worked out for that. I'll tell you more about it tomorrow, when I acquaint you with what's left of my world."

"Can I ask you one vital question?" I earnestly asked. After an approving nod from the alien I continued. "How are you going to explain to your compatriots the fact that your craft is shored up with manmade parts?"

"That's the easiest part. We will move our ship close to one of our outposts and then send a transmission stating that our onboard computers have shut down. We will then transport our crew down to the out post and detonate the ship before the reactors become critical. The ship will be destroyed, along with all traces of our past endeavors. The crew will most likely receive commendations for jobs well done, and I might even get a promotion for my valiant role in all of this. As far as the Captain and the crewmembers that were killed, well, there are always those that will not part with the ship. This is perfectly legal in our society." The alien sat down in the chair behind his desk and smiled at me.

"Is it worth risking your life for? I mean you could go back at any point in time, or you could be engulfed by the void and end up plummeting towards the center of the black hole as a high-density particle."

"You are correct. But it is the only alternative open to us at this time."

"I don't understand you. You go out searching for life, yet your own life means little to you. It doesn't seem logical." The alien knew how hard it was for me to visualize such a lifestyle, but he had little to offer to soothe my thoughts.

"I believe in India, they have concepts similar to ours. John are you familiar with them?" I nodded affirmatively. "Then you know that they believe that this life is not important, for the next will be better. I don't think that I will be reincarnated as they believe, but I do believe that the essence of me will always exist; and therefore, I can take the risk. Not only I, but also my entire race believes in this concept as well. It has brought us a long way. So to us, the void will be a great opportunity to test our theory and we regard it as such,"

Silence ensued for a brief moment as I regarded the alien man so alike and yet so different from myself. I noted the almost perfect mask of serenity settled on his features and the relaxed non-aggressive posture while he sat in his chair. I knew this alien was totally enthralled with the idea of testing his new theory and flirting with death, but then there were few scientists of my own caliber who wouldn't also jump at the same chance.

"And the probabilities?"

"Twenty percent chance that we will not make it out of the black hole, twenty percent chance that we will pass through and go back in time, and a sixty percent chance that we will go through the void, unharmed, and have to try it at least a few more times." I lifted my eyebrows and cast the alien a dubious look.

"At least the odds are in your favor."

"It appears that way, but we won't know until we try it.

Now if you will excuse me, I'd like to go and do some work before I take you along with me tomorrow. I have to inform the rest of the crew about you."

"Until tomorrow." I turned and walked out of the room. I knew I would need a good night's sleep for what tomorrow's surprises might have in store for me.

Sleep would not come easy to me. I turned over and over in every conceivable position. Images of Bill, Julie, and the alien as Dr. Slatski, constantly interchanged with one another, forcing me to contemplate one or several situations, all at the same time. The issues were randomly selected and sometimes had little to do with reality, but they were all time consuming, and kept me awake. Two main topics repeated themselves, one dealt with the alien's way of life and values. The second, what Bill was scheming? Visions of him running into the alien encampment with the probe under his direction, had endless bad out comes. Sometimes he used the probe to crush the aliens, other times the arms of the probe were used to capture them alive. In any case, my gut feelings told me that restraint nr Bill's part couldn't be counted on. The impression was so overwhelming that I finally could not stay in bed any longer. I got dressed and headed down to cargo hanger 2.

It was after two in the morning by the time I arrived at the hangar. I had originally wanted to go in, make some adjustments on the probe that would transmit video of the hangar's users for a few days, but as I stepped through the door, I quickly changed my mind.

"Come right in, you're just in time to see your friends stealing the latest shipment of cargo that they requested."

I was dumbfounded. I walked up to the viewing screen to check for myself. I knew that Bill wouldn't kid around about this, but just in case . . .

"I thought it wouldn't be here for at least another day or so?"

"I moved the deadline. I wanted to see how flexible they were, and boy, was I right. That Dr. Slatski is one smooth operator."

"What's the next move?"

"You'll just have to wait and see, but as always, you'll have to keep this to yourself." Bill looked at the screen as he talked, watching the aliens' steady progress of pilfering in the other cargo bay. The screen's luminescent glow reflected off his eyes giving them a demonic appearance. I felt my stomach painfully twist.

"You mean there might be someone else who would believe me in the first place?"

"You know what I mean."

Both men watched the screen silently; both contemplating the other and the aliens. Soon the cargo bay was picked clean, deserted, and with only empty pallets lying on the floor.

"Well, I've seen enough." I walked away from the viewing port yawning.

"By the way, what made you come down here in the first place?" Bill asked.

"I had this dream that the probe was being stolen, and I had to come down and check on it." I wasn't use to lying, but I thought I sounded convincing.

"You can rest assured that it's safe. I'll be keeping a close eye on it until tomorrow."

"What do you mean, until tomorrow?"

"I haven't had the chance to tell you, but I'm leaving for New York in the morning. My replacement should be here by tomorrow night." I eyed him narrowly, that's very odd, but I wasn't going to question him. Bill seemed to tell you exactly what he thought you should know, and no amount of questioning would gain me further information.

"Well, have a nice flight Bill. Perhaps we shall see each other again." I caught Bill's nod of affirmation as he walked through the open doorway. I certainly couldn't say that I was going to miss him. So I said as little as possible then shortly left the room myself to go back to bed.

Sleep came to me easier knowing that Bill was leaving. I couldn't figure out why, for it seemed to go against Bill's nature. However, government matters had always been mysterious to me and most likely it would remain so in the future. The main thing now was that the aliens could proceed on schedule and I would become privy to knowledge as of yet undreamed of by other men.

PAGE 205

The next morning I didn't need an alarm clock. I had already adjusted to Expom's time zone. The time was eight o'clock. I was supposed to meet the alien down at locker room C within the hour. This gave me more than enough time to shower, shave, and as always, find somewhere nearby to eat. This morning I even had time to try something new, so I went to a quick little restaurant called "Yoshinoyas" or called "The Beef Bowl" by westerners. The place wasn't actually new, for I had eaten at the Beef Bowl in several cities in Japan. It was just that eating Japanese fast food for breakfast on the moon was a combination even I couldn't resist.

The restaurant had a small Japanese setting on the outside, with familiar smells emanating from within. I lowered my head and passed under the small banners that hung at the entrance of the door. Once inside, I was shocked to see the amount of Japanese tourists huddled at the long table and tiny stools. Almost every stool was occupied, elbow-to-elbow, in typical Japanese style. Among the variety of faces I could not see one other non-Japanese. They were an interesting lot I remembered. If they were in Australia, they ate Japanese food. If they went to Germany, they ate Japanese food. I was convinced that no matter where they went, they could find Japanese food. They seemed so unrelenting in their pursuit to keep everything the same wherever they went, but I wasn't really one to talk, after all, I was the king of fast food. So after my short observation, I went over to an unoccupied seat and sat down.

"Ookii beefu boru," I shouted out to the waiter at the far end of the counter. Within seconds, the waiter returned with a big bowl of rice. On the top of the rice, was a mixture of thin strips of beef and slices of onions, all covered in a light brown semi-sweet sauce. I reached for a pair of chopsticks that stood upright in an open jar and I began to voraciously attack the meal like the rest of the patrons. It only took minutes before I had devoured the meal and sat back in retrospect while drinking a cup of green tea. It was as good as in Japan, I thought, I should have come here sooner. I

116

was too full for another bowl, so after another cup of tea I was ready to leave.

"Sayonara, Mata-irashai," echoed the words behind me as I lowered my head to pass under the banners and out the door. "Good-bye, come back again." They really did their best to make it authentic, I thought.

"Hello," I shouted out as I made my way into the locker room. Dean and Garret were just finishing suiting up.

"Where are you two off to?"

"We haven't seen you for a while." Garret said as he finally managed to get his helmet secured in place, and now he could see me clearly. Dean had his helmet on properly, but still had his mouth full. Probably had half his breakfast inside that suit, I imagined. "We're going to try out the jet packs today. Do you want to join us?"

"I wish I could Garret, but I'm all tied up until tonight."

"We understand," Dean said as he cleared his throat.

"You've got another hot date."

"Well, how about tonight then?" Garret quickly added.

"Sounds good, I'll see you then."

The two of them left for the shuttle. I went to my locker, checked my equipment once again, and suited up. By the time I was ready, the alien, Dr. Slatski, came through the shuttle doorway into the locker room. He stood motionless for a minute and looked at me.

"Are you ready to go?"

"Two weeks ago!"

"Let's hurry and make this shuttle then." The alien turned and headed out, I was right behind him.

"Let's get in the last compartment. It's the emptiest of the three. When we get to the end of the moonrail, we'll switch over to the lunar land rover. It'll take us to the end of the ridge, and we will walk from there." I followed silently behind him.

At the end of the moonrail, just as the alien had said, was a lunar land rover. We waited for the tourists to enter into the moon cave and as the last one left the top of the steps to pass inside, we made our way to the rover. It was a two-seater, nothing fancy, similar to the ones used by the early astronauts. We both buckled in. The alien put his feet on the pedals and sped off. First the wheels grumbled as they shot twenty-foot plumes of dust up into the almost non-existent atmosphere. However, plumes quickly reduced in size as the rover approached its maximum speed. Soon we had crossed the edge of the mountain and we were heading in the direction of the far end side, and although we were still on the valley floor, I was certain that we would have to start our ascent up the side of the mountain any minute now, but much to my expectations we never did. The alien kept heading towards the base of the far corner. Finally, he began slowing down, and came to rest not far from the far end. I was glad the tedious ride had ended. My butt was sore from the constant bouncing, and I couldn't wait to set foot on firm ground, even if it had a reduced gravitational field. I was curious, however, for I had climbed this part of the mountain during my earlier excursion, and at that point in time, I had found nothing.

"The opening can't be up there, I've already searched the entire area!"

"And you are right. Now if you will follow me please." He began walking away from the base of the mountain, with me close behind. He stopped in the middle of a barren part of land. "This is it. By standing motionless at this spot for approximately ten seconds, you will feel the ground beneath you move."

I looked down at the moon's dust that encircled his feet. There was no evidence to support his claim, with not one single marker close by to distinguish this spot from any other. Then to my amazement, the ground began to move. Us, along with ten square feet of ground around us, began to descend below the surface. It was like going down an elevator shaft without rigid inner walls or bars to hang onto. As I looked up a new roof closed up overhead and I felt quite insecure. Having descended some fifty feet, the platform underneath our feet came to rest flush with the floor of a long dark tunnel system.

"This way," the alien motioned. I was quick to follow.

"I don't see any sentries."

"We're not exactly at war. Besides, we can't afford the so-called manpower.

"How did you know where to stand?"

"Our sense of acuity along with our vision is better adapted than yours. To us it is as plain as the outline of a crab hiding in the sand. Perhaps as your race evolves, you will accumulate the same abilities."

I decided to not ask any more questions for the time being as I didn't relish the idea of my race being cut down in stature with each and every answer. I also felt that the alien was receiving too much pleasure from such comments. We continued down the corridor, the light was illuminated enough to find ones footing.

"Around the bend and you should be able to get a glimpse of our ship." Then as we turned the corner, a couple of narrow vertical slits in the sidewall of the tunnel permitted a dim yet discernable view. I stopped for a brief second to peer through an opening, and then raced ahead to catch up with the alien who had not slowed down his pace in the least. Dim as it was, I could still see the outline of the scout ship sitting in the middle of a large cavern. I could see figures scurrying from one point to another, but with the existing light, I might as well have been in a subway tunnel, trying to see what was down at the other end of the track. Soon we escaped the eerie darkness and came out into the main cavern. We were only fifty feet from the entrance of the scout ship, and for the first time I could actually perceive how large the ship was. It was enormous, over thirty feet tall, and over seventy feet long. The entire ship was one massive work of art. I could immediately see where the original blast had gnawed away at pieces of the ship, but the crude, irregular welding lines, still did not detract from the overall image. I was overwhelmed.

"Would you like to take it out for a spin?" The alien was obviously amused. "I got that phrase out of the auto magazine." He proceeded to the ship with me close by his side.

Several members of the crew looked up briefly from their assigned tasks. We advanced up a long ramp on the side of the ship. At the top of the ramp, the wall separated and we went inside what appeared to be a holding room.

"This will only take a second," the alien stated. Two sets of doors slid shut behind us and I could hear the sound of some type of gaseous atmosphere rushing in to fill the room.

"You can take your helmet off now." I watched the alien begin to remove his, and then I followed suit.

"That feels more like it. I can't stand these restricting archaic helmets." He pointed towards me. "You have to try on one of ours before you go." I smiled and nodded in agreement. "We'll leave our suits here." came a renewed authoritarian voice. I watched as the alien opened up a side panel on the wall and placed his helmet in one of two small box-like spaces. He then opened up another compartment and began pulling the top part of his suit over his head. When he had finished setting his pants and boots into the compartment, he stood in gray rubber soled socks and green jogging suit, and patiently waited for me to dress down too. Upon seeing my bright orange colored jogging suit, the alien almost broke out in laughter for it seemed so out of place here on his ship. I felt uneasy and instinctively reached down my sides to recheck that my zipped pockets were sealed closed. The alien then proceeded through a doorway, where only seconds before stood a barren wall, and walked off down the corridor. It was narrow and reminded me of a submarine that I once had the pleasure to visit. The submarine's tiny hallways filled one's nostrils with the over powering smell of fresh paint, and the walls reverberated even the most remotely audible sounds. This corridor, on the other hand, had the sterility of a computer chip factory without even the slightest detectable level of scents or sounds. I reached out to touch the wall of the corridor in order to get a feel for the material that was incorporated, and something completely unexpected happened. Instead of my fingers coming into contact with a solid surface, I found my hand moving through a layer of air. The alien noticed my actions and he was amused by the expression of disbelief on my face.

"You just put your hand through the doorway to our environment room. We'll be coming back to that area later. As you have noticed, we manipulate light to give one the impression that a door is present; when in reality you can walk right through. Not only is it maintenance free, but it is also more sound proof than a conventional door." I was impressed, and I immediately thought of how I would utilize such a system in my own laboratory. "Of course with your human vision, you might find it difficult to detect the slight nuance that makes the outline recognizable." My feelings of delight vanished quickly. I was right. The doorway was indistinguishable from the rest of the hallway. At the end of the corridor, we turned to the left and went through another doorway. This time a physically solid door closed behind us. I looked on as the alien placed his hand on a panel on the sidewall. I stood motionless for a brief second. I could detect no movement, but I somehow knew that we were in an elevator. The doorway opened and the two of us walked out into a room

"This is the main navigation center. I believe you would call it the command center."

I half expected to see Spock and Captain Kirk sitting at the helm, but instead what I saw were four empty chairs situated in a semi-circle in the middle of the room, facing eight glassy walls. Not the most impressive sight that I could have imagined. I wanted to see electronics that looked like Apple Computers had merged with Playstation's Wii system. I wanted to see joystick stations that were somehow connected to large wall mounted plasma screens. I wanted to see something I could control with my bare hands.

"All the screens are voice activated, we haven't had to depend on manual control or anything resembling buttons, for over five thousand years." It was like he was reading my mind. "Every command is fed into the computer and the orders are carried out instantaneously. However, there is one disadvantage, if the computer system feels like it, it may override my orders, but this seldom occurs and only when the safety of the ship is concerned. Otherwise I have complete control."

"Then how did you manage to come to the moon in the first place?" The alien smiled, reflecting the tough job it was to interfere with the onboard computer system.

"Any computer program can be changed, any security system can be breached. It is simply a matter of time and manipulating the motherboard, altering resident memory, and redirecting the useful purpose of a few logic circuits."

"And hoping that you don't get yourself killed in the process!"

"You might say that. Here, I'll place some readouts on the screens so you can see for yourself what the computer system can do." He paused as he thought of an appropriate topic. Then in an unfamiliar tone of voice he began. The language was more than foreign to my ear. I doubted that I could even come close in pitch or such harsh sounding tones, let alone the context. Suddenly, as soon as the alien uttered a sound, certain sections of the walls lit up in different shades and patterns; all with strangely uniform subtitles lying directly below or to the side of each and every individual visualization. Out of the entire group there was only one that I could come close to discerning, and that was a picture of Earth. Probably a basic function of this computer, I thought, but the resolution was absolutely life-like or world like in this instance. The image of Earth appeared to be in front of a dark wall, and seemed to be revolving. I was deeply impressed.

"I thought that I would start off with something familiar. Now I'll show you a map of the proposed flight path through the outer ring of the black hole that we have chosen." He softly spoke his commands out loud and several walls simultaneously erased the old information and replaced them with pictures and symbols, with no discerning time lapse between.

"I realize that not being able to read the information may be frustrating, but I at least thought that you should see this." I could only see the Earth and it's moon. An elliptical line extending away from the planet, went through the outer ring of the black hole, and then returned toward the Earth.

"But I thought that you were going home?" I asked.

"We eventually will, but there are three reasons why we are returning here first. When we go through the ring nothing may happen. In that case, we will return and try again at the same starting point. If, on the other hand, we do indeed break the time barrier, then we have no way to accurately predict what period of time we will enter. We may only gain a few days or we might go back centuries. So using Earth as a point of reference, and using our advanced technical abilities, we can ultimately compensate in either direction."

"That sounds good, but what was the third reason?"

"That I was hoping to inform you of later, but you might as well know now. It will not change the course of events." I was extremely confused by the alien's verbosity, and I had a bad feeling the something was not quite right. I hated that feeling of impending doom. Now I wasn't sure I wanted to know the aliens third reason. The alien read the play of emotions crossing my face. He surmised by my expression that now was the time to reveal a little more of his plans. "You see, before the real Dr. Slatski died, we made a bargain with him, that we would presently like to extend to you Dr. Wilson. Dr. Slatski was more than intrigued with our culture and our technology. He did not want us to leave him behind when we left. So we figured out a way for him to go with us. At the time we only had plans for founding a new colony somewhere away from the rest of our race, so there was no major objections to his wishes. When he died though, so did some of our goals; he was very much a part of us. His influence kept our spirits up, and gave us hope for the future. However, with our new plan, he couldn't have gone with us anyway." The alien stopped to catch his breath. Speaking the human tongue for great lengths of time was tiring. Taking a break also gave him a chance to see what kind of emotional progress he was making with me. He looked deeply into my eyes.

"We want to know if you would like to come with us? Because if we are successful and do indeed go back in time, you may have a chance to alter your Earth's entire history. Think of it, you could be instrumental in the revolution of Earth's sciences. By going back a mere three years, would be enough to claim the break through of heavy gravity, or you could bring forth other technological advancements that we could provide you with."

My fear was complete; I never dreamed that the aliens would want to take me with them. Images of Islands with white sand, my laboratory, my studies, and my life's work passed through my mind. The probability that I would never return to have these things was too great a price for me to relinquish lightly.

"Why can't you provide me with that knowledge now, if you're so willing to help out Earth?" The constriction of my windpipe didn't help with my delivery.

"I was offering a gift to you, not Earth. Everything has its price; you have to take the risk with us. If we fail, we may need your help in existing on a part of Earth that is relatively isolated." I knew I had to get off the ship immediately, my stomach burned with tension, but I had to play this game right, the wrong move might cost me my life. Like a chess player maneuvering his opponent into checkmate, I began.

"Frankly, I think that you'll never make it through the ring alive, but your proposition is interesting, and I'll give it a great deal of thought." I held my breath, what would the alien do with this polite refusal? I could feel vibrations emanating from the alien.

Were they based on tension, anger, or appeasement? What would be his next move?

"Very well, I'll give you some time to think it over, but I'll try and persuade you by showing you what your own world could possess with a little outside help." The tension in the air quickly evaporated. I could once again breath and I visibly relaxed. The alien's keen hazel eyes noted this with discernable satisfaction. You are very inexperienced at this game my friend, the alien thought. I will easily win in the end. Although, maybe not exactly as I had planned. He was relieved that humans did not have the ability to detect chemical changes in others, or in essence read minds, although it would have created more of a challenge for him. He walked back to the elevator with me following.

"Next we will go by the reactor, followed by the environmental room." The elevator stopped and the door opened. I perceived this to be the bottom level of the ship, my intuition on locations was usually correct, no doubt helped by the countless years of cave diving. When the only air around was on your back or at the surface, you had to develop a sixth sense for knowing where you were at all times. Having a rope to guide you in dark muddy or clear water was a must, and the rope trail was always right, but it didn't always give one hundred percent assurance like knowing where you were, and the less assured you were, the faster you went through your air supply.

"This is our reactor. Unlike your reactors, this one works by fusion." The idea of fusion had been in the minds of men for several decades, but none had ever succeeded in harnessing such a device. The benefits were incalculable, but still the risk of accompanying the alien was not worth it. I did, however, have to admit that the housing of the reactor was quite impressive. Long thick clear plastic tubes were clustered in uniform groups around the walls. Some of the tubes contained a plasmatic fluid that varied in color, while others emitted flashing particles of light. How it worked would have to remain a mystery to me for now.

"Think of it, given the fundamentals of this reactor, you could accelerate man's technology over night."

"And if you don't make it back in time? Then what? Even if you traveled close to the speed of light, the trip would take so long that by the time you returned, the Earth would have already invented the fusion reactor without your help."

"That could happen, if we didn't break the time barrier, but even then the probability would be low because we will be traveling faster than the speed of light. I'd like to show you the environmental room now."

As we walked out the doorway, I immediately recognized the barren corridor. I tried to strain my eyes to discern the outline of the doorway to the environmental room, but I could not.

"How soon will you be ready to leave?" I asked.

"Soon." I watched the alien turn mid-stride and seemingly walk into the wall, it appeared to envelope his body, and then he was gone. I reached out my hand to sample just what had happened. My hand disappeared with no ill effect, so I moved forward through the doorway. As I came through the other side, I saw the alien stoically standing, waiting for me. I felt rather foolish, but I wouldn't admit it to the alien!

"What keeps your people from running into each other as they pass through the from the opposite side at the same time?"

"By the color of the doorway." All I could see was a barren white wall, so the color of the wall meant nothing to me. After learning this piece of information, the other questions I was going to ask lost their significance. I mean how could I keep asking questions, when the answers meant so little to my understanding of the alien's world. I was visually challenged here. Was it the same for my other senses? The room that I was standing in resembled a locker room, but instead of small metal lockers, there stood lockers seven feet high, by two feet wide, framed with clear glass panels.

"There are more of these on the other side of the ship. That is where the rest of the crew is being kept until needed." The alien opened up one of the containers and I peered inside. A cushion lined the back wall. Electronic devices were precariously positioned under a plastic grid on the floor as well as on the ceiling. The color of the interior was gray except for the cushion, which had a pale orange overtone. So far, the only room that I had seen that fulfilled my need for aesthetic coloration was the reactor room. Then I remembered that there was abundance of color, but not at the level for human appreciation. I wondered if all the loud extravagant colors that humans surrounded themselves with, gave the aliens headaches?

"All you have to do is enter inside, and the computer will see that your time spent in suspended animation is comfortable." He motioned for me to venture inside. I hesitantly accepted the offer. I stepped inside and turned so my back would face the cushion. I noted that the unit was quiet, but the cushion was extremely uncomfortable.

"It certainly isn't made for humans!" I stated, trying to keep the relief out of my voice.

"As a matter of fact, we do have one made for a human, we specifically built one for Dr. Slatski. The critical aspect was recalibrating the unit to accommodate the metabolic functions of a human. Follow me and I'll show you what I mean." He motioned for me to follow him down the aisle. My sense of uneasiness quickly returned, I knew the game was on once again. I regrettably followed, desperately thinking of a way to get off the ship without offending the alien and making it appear that I would consider their offer. Suddenly the alien looked over his shoulder, then turned around, I followed suit and noted another alien walking toward us. The figure was still wearing his helmet and trim lined space suit. Dr. Slatski rapidly spoke using his native tongue. The subordinate stood frozen for a split second, then left as silently as he had entered. I hoped the aliens could not read my mind; it would be too much to know that the alien knew how terrified and desperate I was becoming.

"It appears that we were followed."

"It couldn't be Bill Nico. He said that he was leaving today for Earth."

"It appears that we both have underestimated him. Fortunately, the electrical equipment that he tampered with was easy to repair."

We continued walking down the corridor; my thoughts turned to what Bill was possibly up to now. Bill was much too close, and these aliens had to get away before Bill got his hands on them.

"I need to know exactly how long it will be before you are able to leave?"

"Very soon we hope. As a matter of fact, there is only one thing left to be done." This did nothing to reassure my increasingly negative feelings. We had reached the end of the hall, and the alien opened a door to one of the units. By the shape of the cushion I could tell that this was designed for a human. I didn't dare look closely at the interior, for my unsettling feeling had begun to permeate my body. I could feel it flowing outward and engulfing the room.

"With what you have seen and been told, will you join us?" The alien softly spoke as he looked deeply into my eyes, as if with eye contact alone he could persuade me. I felt the alien's body absorbing my vibrations of terror as if trying to ease me into a relaxed state.

"Even though you offer all this, I still have to refuse. I enjoy my present lifestyle, I don't have the time or energy to reshape the world, nor do I want to. I enjoy being a scientist in my own age and time. Besides, few men ever appreciate what is given to them, things have far more value when they are earned."

"While noble, I'm disappointed to hear what you say, because the environmental chamber works more efficiently when the individual inside is in a relaxed state." All my fear turned to rage, they would not take me against my will, I would fight with my very last breath. I could hardly speak because of anger, but I managed to spit out words through gritted teeth.

"Perhaps you didn't understand me. I'll help you here on the moon, but under no circumstances do I wish to risk my life to join you in testing your lunatic theory." Suddenly, before I could continue my verbal attack, the entire ship began to shake, we both dropped to bent knee stances, but were still hard pressed to keep our balance.

"What was that?" I yelled at the alien.

"I believe we were hit by one of your primitive weapons."

"But how did they find their way through the tunnels?"

"We're not in the tunnels." A flush of red filled my face as I asked the question to which I had already guessed the answer.

"Then where are we?"

"A thousand miles farther away as each second passes."

I clenched my right fist and brought it smashing towards the alien's face, but something was not right, the alien was able to grasp my fist in time and thwart my effort. I was now aware of what had gone wrong. I had been drugged. I couldn't figure out how or when, but a lighthearted feeling was taking over my body and increasing steadily in strength. In a dream like state I felt my moon suit separating from my body and wearing nothing but my space suit undergarment I floated inside the chamber. I came to rest with my back against the cushion. I was growing weak, but some kind of attraction force emitted by the cushion kept my body in an upright position. My thoughts began to drift away. Soon my eyelids became too heavy and slid shut like blast furnace doors.

"Rest easy my friend," were the last words I heard before succumbing to an overpowering deep sleep.

Page 225

Bill watched the two of us leave as he had anticipated. By the use of bugging devices, which he had installed in my room and Dr. Slatski's office, he had advance knowledge of what Dr. Slatski's next move would be. From listening to the conversations, he was also able to ascertain that the aliens wanted nothing whatsoever to do with the planet Earth. His job would be to persuade them otherwise. He knew this endeavor might be fruitless, but armed with the information that the aliens were not even in contact with their own race Bill had formulated a plan. If the aliens would not cooperate he rationalized, then they would have to be exterminated. Dr. Slatski was no exception as far as Bill was concerned. He still couldn't believe he had been fooled by the alien's human charade. He really was only after their technology in the first place, the social benefits that they could give Earth, would be shelved for some other time. This was not only his opinion, but that of his superiors as well. The trick, however, was to steal their technology without their comrades back home realizing what they had done. At least not until the new technology had become well entrenched in Earth's society. He and a small group of soldiers were now positioned inside the remnants of a crater. The crater was located halfway between the moonrail station by the moon cave, and the edge of the mountain ridge. They watched through their binoculars as Dr. Wilson and the alien roared past them, using the undomesticated moon rover. As soon as we had passed, under the guise of the rover created dust clouds, Bill moved his group and followed behind.

Our vehicle easily out distanced them, and by the time we had reached the edge of the mountain, Bill was by design just approaching the far side of the mountain. The back up rover Bill's team was using to bring the probe was even slower. They had already noted the position where our rover came to rest, and where we had gotten out and started walking. The driver hauling the probe, was doing his best, but was having some sort of mechanical issues. The probe in general had not changed since it's near demolition in the storage bay, the lens was still cracked, and the silver material had not been cleaned off, although the substance had lost its original luster, but one thing was different. Strapped to the top of it stood a long cylindrical object. Bill had predicted that the aliens would soon be ready to leave with the stolen materials that they had utilized. He had also conceived that if it had been the detonation of the R.E.D.s device that had originally crippled the alien vessel, then the duplication of such misfortune should further delay if not permanently ground their ship. They would have the choice of either giving up their technology outright, or die trying to conceal it. The plan was good, simple, and did not endanger too many of his own men. He did however; regret the fact that Dr. Wilson might not survive the explosion. He was sure that by now the aliens had told him many useful things about themselves.

        The alien and I stopped. Bill squinted his eyes as he brought the details of our helmets into focus. The binoculars he was using were a bit awkward to maneuver with his heavy gloves, especially when pressing the buttons to change the focal point. He found he was squinting while trying to resolve in fine detail the outline of our helmets. The act of squinting was a carry over from his years of service with the F.B.I.; too many late night stakeouts he thought. He went back to concentrating on the two figures that appeared on the screen of the tiny box that had replaced the old version of binoculars with the two eyepieces to look through. Of course, with a life support helmet on, the old style would not have helped him see our faces anyway. There was something to be said for it though, for with the two telescopic tubes connected by a central ridge, the possible ways of manipulation were endless, but with the modern wedge shaped version with the screen at one end and a narrow curvature at the other end, there was no practical way to keep the slippery devil in your hands; even if they were sticky. So he bitched, moaned, and continued observing.

        "I'll be," he whispered. He turned to two of his men carrying another telescopic instrument that had the appearance of a shoulder held rocket launcher. "Get a mark on that position and get ready." The two men quickly obeyed his orders. One of them braced the launcher across his shoulder while looking through a small screen. The other one raised the back end of the four-foot long tube to help stabilize it. My outline appeared near the center of the screen. A built in crossbar on the screen flashed as I became precisely centered in. The man pressed a button and a fixed digital readout on my position appeared in the upper left hand corner of the screen. The readout quickly began to vary.

"I can't keep it steady," the soldier said into his helmet microphone.

"It's alright, I only wanted the initial readout." Bill watched as the figure of myself and that of the alien descend beneath the surface. Soon we were gone and a hole had taken our place. Bill waited patiently for the ground to return in place and the hole to disappear from view.

"Alright men. You five come with me, and you three stay here with the launcher. Set it up on the tripod, and get it ready. If you see anything bigger than a lunar rover come into view, blast it! I repeat, don't wait for us, and just blast it. You may only get one chance." He turned his attention to the five soldiers he had selected. They had all heard his last statement, and were not overly enthused about blasting potential tourists, but to them orders were orders.

"Hand me my flight pack," he directed one of the men. Quickly he was given a compact pack with two tiny rocket motors, one on each side of the pack. With the help of the soldier, he rapidly placed it over his breathing backpack unit, fastened the waist strap, and brought the two side arm control bars around to his chest.

"Ready men?" He squeezed the handle grip controls, and in unison a nodded reply came back to him; they simultaneously lifted off. The jet packs that they wore were smaller than the Earth version, with good reason. With the decreased amount of gravity, a smaller amount of power was required to move them about. Once the men had reached a height of thirty feet, they leveled off and made some quick adjustments. Thirty feet was the standard height for military operations, any higher and you risked long-range detection and used too much fuel to cover any appreciable distance. Any lower, and you ran the risk of raising the surface dust in front of your vision or running into unforeseeable objects. Everything seemed secure, so off the troops went in the shape of a V-formation following close behind Bill.

Traveling at high speed above the surface they were able to complete the journey in less than a few heartbeats. Bill signaled the group to land about fifty feet from the readout hotspot. As they descended, a huge dust cloud began to envelope them. Bill could not see his feet hit the surface, but the sudden jolt on his ankles and kneecaps told him that he had landed. He was standing in an orange colored soup bowl. He knew that there was a man directly behind him, and one ten feet to his left and also on his right, but he could see none of them. He had to act swiftly, he released himself from the rocket pack, dropped it by his side, and began to run-hop forward. If he had hesitated for even a moment, he might have found himself under the feet of the man directly behind him. The two men in back would have the worst go of it if they became misaligned, for they would end up stumbling over the other men's jet packs, and ending up face first in the dust, but since time was critical, this seemed to be the preferred method of conducting such a maneuver on the moon. On the down side, the jet packs could have easily malfunctioned, and one jet pack refusing to extinguish while the men tried to carry out their assigned tasks would have given way to disastrous consequences. Plus, an enemy force could have shot them down like flies, as the men literally groped around in the dark. But none of this took place. Bill stopped thirty feet from where he had landed and turned back to observe. All the packs had shut off properly, and the dust was gently settling. His men had had no problems and were spreading out behind him. For once, he had been sent the best he thought to himself. He signaled them to regroup and they walked to the position that the readout had indicated.

The three men left behind with the launcher confirmed Bill's position. They stood motionless and waited. Bill was not sure if the ground would move for him the way it had for the alien, but he was willing to try it out. Perhaps it worked automatically like an elevator door and he could enter undetected or perhaps it had to be activated by someone inside, in which case they would be surrounded or worse within seconds.

To his amazement something began to happen.

"Steady men." He yelled as he saw them bringing their guns into firing position. The men were apprehensive and becoming defensive was their natural reaction. To another army, Bill thought, they might have looked impressive, but against aliens with advanced weaponry, he was not sure if his men could be valued little more than aesthetically pleasing. This is what it must have felt like to the Aztec warriors going against armored horse riding Spanish soldiers. This was one reason behind bringing so few along, when in fact; even a large force would find itself overwhelmed by the military power of an advanced alien race. Still he permitted them to bear arms, in order to give them a false sense of security.

As the ground beneath them lowered, the men crouched down. They were looking for signs of posted sentries. Fortunately, the tunnel below was unguarded. The men still had no idea what they were looking for, so they had no reason to sigh in relief as Bill did, when he had assured himself that the area was deserted. Every move he made would be a gamble. He had hopes of finding aliens, giving them his ultimatum, and after that it was anybody's guess what would happen. He only hoped that he would still be alive when all was said and done. It was a quick way to fame and fortune, or a quick way to end his life. The latter alternative he tried to ignore. The platform beneath them finally came to a stop. They at least build nice elevators, he acknowledged as he noticed that the materials incorporated in the structure were the property of Expom. The bright yellow Expom trademark was clearly visible on several of the support beams. With little chance of the structure ever being discovered, the aliens would naturally have had little need for covering up such markings. Stepping away from the elevator, he proceeded down the tunnel with his men close behind. They were all curious as to why an Expom elevator was situated in such a remote spot, but Bill was not about to attempt any explanation. They followed the dark tunnel until it came to a fork in the road as it were. Bill was uncertain as to which path to follow, so he reached into one of his side pockets and pulled out a flashlight. He lit up the dark cavern to examine the two alternatives. Both had signs of heavy use and footprints that looked similar. This was the frustrating part, if he guessed wrong, they could spend an extra hour or so searching in possibly the wrong direction. So in order to be certain, he got on his hands and knees and carefully scrutinized the prints.

"We'll go this way," he affirmatively announced as he raised himself back off the ground and headed down the branch that lead to the right. It turned out to be the correct choice, for he was soon stopping and looking through the same cracks of the tunnel wall that Dr. Wilson had recently peered through. He had also arrived just in time to, see one of the aliens walking up the ramp into the ship. As Bill reached the opening to the huge cavern, the ramp was being raised into its take off position and secured flush against the side of the ship.

"What in God's name is that?" One of the men asked. Bill did not even bother to answer, he was awe struck by the sheer size of it all. Then it dawned on him--something very bad. The area was a mess with things discarded everywhere. He had witnessed their meticulous habits as they stole the cargo from Expom. All this scene of rubbish seemed out of place and against the aliens' nature. It looked more like a dumpsite, similar to the ones left behind by the early lunar landers. Without warning, the ship began to produce a low humming sound. These pieces could only add up to one thing, Bill belatedly realized.

"GET OUT. GET OUT OF HERE!"
His men were quick to respond, but by the time they turned around he had already headed back down the tunnel. There was only one place for the ship to go and that was straight up. He figured that the minute the ship broke through the ceiling of the cavern, his men would fire on it with the missile, and he didn't want to be close by when that happened. He moved rapidly through the tunnel trying to keep his feelings of panic in check and never looking back once to see if the men had heeded his orders. He practically flew through the corridor, past the fork, and onto the main tunnel. Several times his arms brushed roughly against the sidewalls, but he managed to keep his pace. As he approached the elevator, a new wave of anxiety took hold of him. How could he lower the elevator? Panic threatened to overwhelm him. This was the closest that he had ever come to death. Standing several feet away from the base of the elevator, he contemplated the situation. This gave the rest of the men a chance to catch up to him, still clasping their heavy, but useless weapons.

"There has got to be a switch or light beam of some sort. If that ship moves before we get out of here, we'll all end up as pieces of moon dust." This prompted the men to look with incredible earnest.

Suddenly, the platform began to descend. Not one of them could have explained why such a phenomenon occurred, they were just grateful that it had. Before the elevator came to a stop, they jumped on board, and stood helpless, waiting for the platform to ascend once again. Bill didn't wait for it to stop at the surface either. He was first off, with the others following a close second. Because he was the only one that didn't have any extra gear to carry, he easily out distanced the others over to the jet packs. The few seconds head start was enough time for him to reach his pack, throw it over his shoulders, and fasten the waist strap. The second man to reach the jet packs was in the process of throwing it over his shoulders, when he saw Bill bringing his handles into position. "No!" the man shouted out, but it was too late. Bill had ignited his rockets and dust was flying everywhere. The other man came at him to stop him, but Bill kicked him out of the way as he shot forward and then up off the ground. The rest of the men, by this point could not see their hands in front of them, let alone find their packs. They began to curse Bill as they dropped to their knees and began a desperate search for the jet packs. The shaking ground beneath them hampered their movements. It began the moment that they had left the platform, but they had not become aware of it until the intensity had increased to the point where they could no longer stand. Bill could hear the rumbling noise as well as the voices of his men over the intercom as they cursed him.

"I'm going to kill that bastard," rang in Bill's ears. Another minute and I'll be free, was his only prevalent thought. He was presently forty feet above the ground and traveling away from the scene fast. Breaking through the thin surface layer proved to be no great task. When the aliens first constructed the makeshift roof, they had designed it with this aspect in mind. As the ship began to break through the ground, the fragmented pieces of rock and debris arched upwards, then gently slid down the sides of the ship toward the bottom of the cavern. The movement of the ground was harmonious, moving in a domino like sequence, the men clinging to the rocks for their lives were the only pieces not seemingly fitting into place. Soon they were tumbling down into the crater that was forming. Simultaneously, the alien ship rose up and cleared the surface.

The three men at the outpost couldn't believe what had transpired before their eyes. They had just witnessed the apparent death of their comrades and the rising of a spacecraft the likes of which; they had never seen before, but still, they were ready for almost anything. When the ship had cleared above the surface, they fired. The man that had pressed the trigger felt a sigh of relief for a fraction of a second, as he saw the red tail of the rocket, as it flew at the ship. A ray of blue light suddenly shot out from the ship and intercepted the missile in mid-flight. The missile exploded close to the ship, but not close enough to do any visible damage. The men ducked for cover in order to avoid any after-shock waves.

Bill was still high above the surface when the explosion occurred; the waves sent him soaring towards the side of the mountain. His hands were literally ripped off of the control handles. He was spinning out of control. Although his rockets were no longer triggered on, his altitude appeared to be increasing. The last thing he saw was a brief glimpse of the ship ascending followed by the side of the mountain rushing towards him. He closed his eyes. The back of his helmet was the first point to hit, immediately producing a loss of pressure in his suit. Next was the jet pack, it crushed inward on his rebreather system and sliced deeply into his spine. The pack imploded and a small fire ignited and was fueled briefly by the remaining air that was rushing out of the suit. Bill felt the pain in his back, then blacked out. He died quickly as the internal organs of his body tried to equalize with the zero atmosphere of the moon.

The three men had raised their heads just in time to witness the explosion that consumed Bill's air supply. They smiled and proceeded to hoof it over to the newly formed crater. They could only hope that the others had somehow survived the ordeal. As for the corpse on the side of the hill, they would leave it till later. Unless anyone looked closely, they would probably overlook Bill for some time to come.

PAGE 238

The alien in charge stood looking at John's motionless body as the second in command approached him with a progress report.

"All in order. Our defense system destroyed a primitive incoming projectile. No damage to the ship." He stood at attention while he waited for the Captain to speak. Dr. Slatski had vanished; in his place was an assertive alien Captain of a re-born ship.

"Excellent. Have the rest of the crew report to their environmental chambers. Soon we will join them."

The second in command was quick to obey. Within minutes the last remaining crew members shuffled through the doorway and advanced down the narrow aisle to their pre-assigned chambers. Silently with much purpose they entered and closed their own doors behind them. Meanwhile the Captain opened the control panel to John's chamber and set the automatic wake up in the off position. He signaled his second in command to enter his chamber, and then paused for a moment to reflect. He had waited a long time to become Captain of a working ship, and it felt good. After his brief pause, he entered his own chamber and settled in for a long needed rest.

The ship was now under the control of a pre-recorded program. The spacecraft began to accelerate after it left the weak gravity field of the moon. Faster and faster the ship continued to travel. As it reached close to the speed of light, the ship began to fade from view, and then it vanished. The ship, along with the occupants, were nothing but a collection of heavy atomic particles soaring in unison through, for all intents and purposes, the empty void of space.

A great deal of time passed since they first began their long awaited journey. The current mission program had almost come to an end, and the ship began to slow down. Soon the ship materialized; the speed of light no longer being exceeded. The Earth and moon could be picked out quite clearly on the screens, but it would still be some time before the crew became active.

The alien Captain was dreaming, but with each passing minute, he found it harder to stay asleep. The force that pulled his back against the cushion began to diminish and he had to stand up in place with the use of his own muscles. The dreams faded, and his eyes opened. He felt fresh and alert, there were no lingering ill effects. He opened the door and stepped out. Soon other crewmembers would do the same. He went over to John's chamber, and was shocked by what he saw. It was obvious that something had gone wrong, for John's face was covered by hair. The hair extended over his forehead and down over his eyes, and was met by a light gray beard strewn with strands of brown hair, which reached down over the collar of his shirt. Although the aging process had not progressed far, it was still remarkable, considering that the aging process even took place at all. The Captain could only hope that internally John was all right. John was more than a man, he was an investment in the future of mankind, and if the Captain was going to help speed up the evolution of man, John would have to survive. His plan was simple, in order for his own race to perceive humankind, as more than a primitive species, man would have to evolve. If he could assist in speeding up the evolutionary developmental process, then he personally could feel responsible for bringing together his ancient cultured race and this newly evolved uncivilized race. Not only would this open up free trade, but it would also alleviate the boredom in life that his own race had encountered over the last mind numbing couple of million years.

He left John's chamber and went to the navigational room. All appeared to be in working order, he orally dispatched several commands and the computer quickly responded. First it confirmed that they had indeed gone back in time. The Captain was overwhelmed with his success, but as the computer scrolled down more information, his mood changed dramatically. They had gone back in time, but the period of time even after the long trip back to Earth, placed them approximately one hundred and seventy thousand years away from where he wanted to be.

"Oh no!" For all intensive purposes, he had failed. By now the rest of his crew were going back to their working positions, and all seemed aware of what had happened. To them however, it was not as important, for they could always return to the chambers and wait, but they had seen the facial effects on the man from Earth, and they immediately knew that for him, the chamber could end up being a death bed if he went one more launch. Much needed to be learned about human longevity and their more primitive yet undeniably similar genetics before time travel would be completely compatible and non-lethal.

The Captain sat in one of the chairs in the navigation room, deep in thought. Beside him, patiently stood his second in command. The options for the Captain to decide John's future were few, actually only two: remain asleep in the chamber for a possible second try, or remain awake on Earth in what he believed was the current Pleistocene era. He stood up in order to view all screens.

"Computer, how many different species of humans exist at this point in time?" Within seconds the data filled the screens. In all there were five distinct separate species according to their classification system with several sub-species all in decline and either relegated to isolated pockets in Asia or remote groups of islands. A genealogical tree appeared on one panel that showed three dominant species with disturbingly high volumes of webs due to cross breeding. Two of the dominant species were still at a very early stage in tool usage, and both were hunter-gatherers. The other group appeared to be more apelike and shorter in stature despite their bipedal stance. It was clear that the information he was going to give John originally would now be of little value. How could these simple-minded creatures build a fusion reactor when the concept of fire was still so relatively new? Absolutely ridiculous, so much for his simple plan concerning the development of man for trading purposes. It was also very clear to him that for John, this would be a very difficult period to survive.

An idea came to mind for the second in command, but he was hesitant to speak up. After all, this was a new Captain and he had been with a few who were not open to suggestions from those of lower rank. Finally, after building up his courage, he offered his suggestion.

"He still might be useful." The Captain looked surprised, but remained silent, and gave him an affirmative nod to continue. "He might be a deciding factor as to which of the two species becomes dominant, or his own genetic makeup could produce yet another dominant species."

He does have a point the Captain thought, not exactly what I had in mind . . .

"He will die if we leave him in the chamber, and in that case, he will have been no use to us at all."

This statement angered the Captain, and he heard the echo of John's words, "I'll not play god with you." It was hard to believe that he was now in just the same predicament? His anger faded to sorrow; he could not let this man die; even as a lesser species, he had come to mean a great deal to the alien. He also felt that he had a debt to repay. Playing the role of Dr. Slatski had affected him emotionally and this could not be tolerated he thought with disgust.

"You are right. Wake him, and prepare to land." The second in command quickly walked away. While he had taken over the role of the human scientist his second in command had become more aggressive. It was a good sign he thought, for he would soon make a fine Captain of his own ship. He turned his attention back to the readouts since his problem with John had been resolved.

I felt myself slowly coming out of my dreams. My arms began to feel very sore, and a terrible acrid smell began to fill my nostrils. In my dream I had been running, my legs were beginning to tire, but I kept on. The smell of sweat permeated my body. My heart hurt, and even though I tried to stop running, I couldn't. I could feel pain radiating up from my toes to the tips of my fingers. As the running continued, I prepared to scream. My mouth tried to open, but even my facial muscles had become swollen and stiff. I felt my body leaning forward. I opened my eyes and saw a door rushing towards my face. I slumped over and fell halfway out of the chamber. I felt two aliens trying to help me stay up. Each time they raised me my sore legs dangled in the air, and then coiled up as my feet collided with the floor.

The smell of the human's body was almost more than the aliens could bear. However they had their orders, and the orders had to be carried out. After some difficulty, they had managed to transport the limp human body over their shoulders down the corridor to a room with a flat horizontal table embedded in the wall. They dropped the body onto the table and closed a lid over him.

By this time, I could see clearly what was happening to me, but my body was too sore to resist. A bank of needles embedded in what looked like a white chalkboard eraser was pressed against my shoulder and the needles penetrated my skin and injected some kind of substances. One of the aliens pushed a button and I felt my body being vibrated. The feeling was welcomed for the pain began to decrease and for the first time since I had entered the chamber, I was able to freely move my fingers, but my legs and arms felt paralyzed. I lay quiet, waiting for the rest of my pain to go away. Soon my facial muscles had relaxed and I found myself moving my lower jaw. I smiled at the aliens.

"That really feels nice." But as soon as I finished this statement I felt a rush of cold water burst against me.

"What the?" I screamed, but the spray continued. The water was coming from several uniformly arranged tiny holes embedded in the sides of the walls. It was so cold that I could hardly stand it. I began beating on the transparent door, while gasping for air. Fortunately the water did not appear to be collecting around me or I would have gone berserk. Suddenly the water stopped and the vibrating waves once again crossed through my body.

"That's more like it," I sighed and in my mind I laid back down on the table. I realized that my clothes were somehow drying with great speed.

"Of course you realize I'm going to break every bone in your bodies the minute I get out of here." The two aliens seemed unmoved by my threat. I looked up at the ceiling while I patiently waited for a chance to rip their throats out, although, I would also have to thank them later for getting rid of my rancid human odor. As I lay there, my face began to itch. It was a strange feeling, one that I hadn't felt in many years. When I eventually able to bring my hand up to scratch, I realized what had happened.

"Son of a..." my voice trailed off in amazement. "Let me out of here," I demanded. "I want some answers, and I want them, now!" The two alien figures ignored me, even as I began to beat my fist against the transparent window. By the time the Captain finally arrived, I was exhausted.

"I've been told that you wish to be let free." I silently stared at him. I was saving up my energy; the minute the door opened I was planning to overpower all three of them. Of course the look in my eyes alone, gave myself away, and the aliens didn't need to use any other senses to know that my potential intent was based on pure unmitigated violence.

"I wouldn't do anything rash my friend. On board I am the Captain, and they will do anything to protect me, even if it means having you killed. I would be unable to stop them as their first duty is to ensure my life regardless of any order I may issue. So may I suggest that you review your position in a logical and rational manner, before we release you." The door slowly opened and I looked out as slowly extended my legs to the edge. My legs were very sore, like I just ran a marathon sore. This was not the time to be macho; I rationalized as I tried to get a hold on my raging anger. I staggered out like a deformed zombie and tried to stand up straight, I could do it, but with more effort than the walking dead. The Captain seemed aware of my condition.

"We still have some work to do before humans will be able to properly use the environmental chambers. My apologies for your discomfort."

"Where are we?"

"Close to Earth."

"Did your theory work?"

"It did, and we soon will be returning home after we return to Earth." I noticed that he showed no emotion whatsoever when stating this fact. This didn't bother me though, as it wasn't the first time that I had seen this emotional difference portrayed in our cultures. I, on the other hand, would have been ecstatic if I had proved such a theory. Why else had I become a scientist if not to test what was and discover what wasn't known?

"We will be landing soon, are you well enough to walk?"

"I think so, where are you taking me? Back to my lab in Fiji?"

"I'm afraid that is out of the question."

"Then where?"

"The computer has selected a remote location." I tried to walk a few steps forward and almost fell. One of the two guards quickly grabbed my left arm to stabilize me.

"Why is my body so weak?"

"Because you almost died. I should have never brought you along, but I felt the advancement of Earth was worth the risk.

"You mean worth risking my life?" The second in command entered the room and spoke briefly to the Captain in the alien dialect.

"I will be going now, my second in command will escort you out off the ship." The Captain quickly turned and left the room. He had indeed changed since he no longer played the role of Dr. Slatski. Absolutely nothing fazed him, I thought as I tried to stop him, but I as I moved, I was swiftly intercepted by the second in command. I could feel the firm grip of his hand, followed by a polite gesture.

"Come with me please." I was just as tall as any of them, and with my past college dabbling in Judo and Kung Fu appearances alone would suggest that I could over power one or two of them, but in my current condition, they had an internal strength far beyond my capacity to confront and overcome. I couldn't even break the firm grip on my arm, so without further struggle I accepted my fate and my muscles relaxed.

"After you," he politely said. The alien let go of my arm and while standing slightly behind me guided me out of the room. The other two guards followed behind us. The three of us made our way to what looked like a small depressurization room that adjoined an air locked exterior door. I could see clouds moving by the tiny porthole. I didn't even notice the entrance door behind us shut, but I felt the pressure change on my ears.

"When will we land?'

"We are landing right now."

"I understood that I was to be given some of your technology?"

"You were, but things have changed. Do to unforeseen circumstances, your race is not yet ready for what we have to offer." I felt that sinking feeling in the pit of my stomach again. They were really trying my patience, but what could I do other than get sick on their boots, I thought as I turned to give the alien a menacing glare.

"Just exactly how far back in time are we talking about here? More than a hundred years?"

"Perhaps, we will have to wait in the chambers until time advances, before we can return home.

"Then why not have me wait in the chamber too? It doesn't make sense to leave me here and now.

"You would not survive. The fact is that you already narrowly escaped death in the chamber. We feel that you could be more useful alive now, than dead in the future."

I couldn't feel the landing, but I could tell by the opening of the ramp entrance that I was soon to disembark. I had to agree that being alive was better than being dead any day, but as the ramp lowered I had second thoughts. A cold wave of air filled the room, and I was instantly chilled to the bone. This was definitely not Fiji. Outside I could see a sparsely populated pine forest heavily endowed with moss.

"Where in the world are you leaving me?" My teeth began to chatter.

"Put these on over yours." I was ordered. I was given back my pair of boots plus the moonsuit that I came aboard the ship wearing. One of the guards had been holding them the entire time, but I had never given it any thought until now. I heartily accepted the outfit and quickly slipped the pants and sweater like top over my own clothes. I was starting to get my muscle movements back under control. I stepped into the boots and within seconds his shivering and teeth chattering stopped.

"I realize that you may not want to land in a populated area, but isn't this just a little bit too isolated?"

"I assure you that it was not our intent. You will find others close by."

"Where am I, and what am I suppose to do here? You owe me that much!" I was getting more agitated by the moment. Then I felt that familiar sleepy feeling overpowering me. It wasn't the chamber that was making me feel week, they were somehow controlling my muscle movements. This time when my strength left me however, I was able to keep my eyes open, but the two guards had to hold me upright as the door to the outside world opened and I was escorted down the ramp. Once past the edge of the ramp, the guards let go of me and I slumped over and went down on the ground. The second in command stood towering over me and looking down at my face.

"If you want to advance your kind, there is only one, very simple thing that you must do. You will quickly figure it out."

With that said he stepped over my inert body and proceeded up the ramp. As the door to the ship's hull closed and the ramp recessed. The sleepy feeling began to pass.

PAGE 250

I lay with my back facing the ship. As my head began to clear, a stream of moss and other bits of debris was deposited on my body. I soon became enveloped in a cloud of smoke. Gasping for air, I curled into the fetal position and covered my mouth and nose with my hands in a futile attempt to filter out the air. By the time I could tolerate breathing again, the ship was gone. All that remained was a singed patch of ground. I was alone, not knowing where I was or where to go. I coughed a few more times, cleared my throat, and rose to my feet. I was standing in a swampy bog-like meadow; most of the trees were dwarf-like and mangled unnaturally. Between the trees were numerous small ponds and springs. Around the edges of the meadow stood a large assortment of pine trees. I noticed that the landscape tended to slant upward, in one direction. Nothing peculiar was visible except that the trees tended to be taller due to the gradual increase in elevation where the ground must have been dryer. There was no steady wind, and with nothing else to guide me, I started walking in the direction of the elevated area. As I approached the first pool of water, my throat became wet with anticipation, but as I leaned over and looked through the water, I could see a host of tiny creatures busily working away. Some were chewing on algae while others were eating whatever swam by. A dragonfly the size of a small bird swooped down and occasionally collected some of the bugs that surfaced for air. I had never seen anything like it before. By the time I reached the edge of the meadow, the sun's heat had begun to take its toll on me. Standing in the shade of a large pine tree, I was able to let the low flowing wind cool myself off. Looking around, I still could see no landmarks to guide me. Behind me lay nothing except underbrush and trees, in front of me was more of the same. It didn't matter which way I went, I was still going to have to fight my way through the underbrush. At first I thought I would have to slash through it all day, but after I had gone some fifty feet, the ground became soft and the underbrush changed from dense clumps of berry bushes to more manageable low lying ferns. I proceeded through the ferns at a fast pace. Spending most of my life near the ocean, I had no idea that this was a bad decision. The ground was gradually becoming softer and softer. Ahead was a thick clustered area of skunk cabbage that gave off a distinct odor that simulated the smell of decaying flesh. I wanted to pass this area quickly, but as I stepped over the first skunk cabbage bush, my boot sank into the mud and my entire body was thrown off balance. Before I had time to become completely aware of what was happening, I was plummeting face first into the mud. I landed hard. Nothing had been hurt, only my pride. The mud was sticky and had a suction-like grip effect on my body. I pushed myself to my knees and wiped the mud away from my face. I was so mad I could scream at the Gods of Olympus, but what good would it do, I thought as I peeled off the offensively stinking dirt. I hoped there would be a town nearby where I could take a hot shower. Slicking back the muddy hair out of my face and beard, I continued my pursuit up to higher ground. For the meantime, I tried to stay out in the open areas between the trees, where the sun's rays could penetrate and help dry me off.

I continued on for over an hour, most of the dried mud had flaked off, but the smell of skunk cabbage still lingered. The gradual sloping of the terrain had long since diminished. I had to climb with the use of my arms, up almost vertical walls grabbing at the roots of trees and branches aided me in my way up what I knew for sure to be the side of a mountain. I still could not be sure where I was going however, for the trees blocked my view, and gave no indication of whether I was correct in my summation.

I had not been on a hike in the mountains since I was a child. The spectacular scenery should have given me much pleasure, but not knowing where I was, preoccupied my thoughts. Just then, a large eagle flew overhead, and a new thought entered my mind. It had been the first time that I had even considered the possibility of encountering wild animals. I was so convinced that I was near civilization, that the thought of even seeing something other than a pigeon had been to remote of an idea to consider. The sight of this bird, however, brought me back down to reality. I had never seen an eagle out in the wild, especially one so big, and where there were eagles, there could just as easily be lions, tigers, or bears. Oh well, at least I thought I was funny considering my current circumstances. The eagle passed by several times. At first it examined me as if I were edible, then it eyed me purely out of curiosity. It probably hasn't seen too many mud monsters, I amusingly thought. I stopped to rest while the eagle circled, and then continued on my way when the bird flew away. Another two hours had passed. I was climbing up the side of a mountain, but could still not see the timberline or any other far away landmarks.

"Blast you trees," I softly uttered. The sound of my voice felt good, and broke the monotony of my quiet surroundings. As I continued up the mountain, my stomach began to growl. I was not used to so much physical exertion without having any snacks to eat along the way. I had earlier passed by some blackberry bushes and now wished that I had brought some with me. Nevertheless, I was not about to turn back yet, because a town, along with a good hot meal, could be just on the other side of the hill. I knew that I had at least twenty dollars in my inner pocket, so as long as they took American money I could buy a big Mac or a double whopper with cheese provided I didn't go back before McDonalds and Burger King first became franchises. Although getting back home to Fiji could prove to be another matter. It all depended on how far back in time they had left me, and how far away was I? I figured that if it were more than a hundred years, then transportation would be by Model A and not by F-150 truck for quite some time. Another hour had passed before I reached the beginning of the timberline. Far to my right I could see the beginnings of distant mountain peaks. The higher ones had snow covering the very tops. I was convinced that I was either in Russia or Canada. I was betting on Canada. At least Canada was closer to my childhood home; the beer with fish and chips was great, and the people friendly if not down right out the friendliest of any country. Russia would have been another story. The food there wasn't my favorite, but with a little vodka life was manageable and easier to make friends.

Ahead I could see what I thought was the top of a mountain. When I reached the summation I found it to be nothing more than the first of many plateaus. Each time I reached a pinnacle, I could see more of the surrounding area, but still not the top or any town in sight. Soon the wind began to pick up and the first signs of snow appeared. A small patch of snow had been melting. The water that ran off formed into a small trickle at the base of the lowest point. A closer look proved that it was not snow at all, but a giant sheet of ice with just a little bit of loose snow lying scattered on top. The wind and melting actions of the sun had transformed the outer edges that had once been lightly packed snow into densely packed ice. I tried to break off a piece of the ice, but found chipping a piece off too difficult, so instead I cupped my hands beneath where the water trickled down from the lowest point of the ice, and waited for the cold water to accumulate in my hands. By the time I had satisfied my thirst, my hands were numb. I must say though that the water tasted rather unfamiliar, as there was no chlorine, chemicals, or other flavor additives, simply a bland refreshing quality. Rubbing my hands together brought back the natural coloration.

I headed up the mountainside again using what appeared to be a deer trail, although, the hoof prints seemed unusually big for deer. They might have been elk tracks for all I knew. The area surrounding the trail slowly slanted uphill. Small blades of grass were dominant. The trees that tried to survive at this altitude were all under a foot tall and appeared close to death. Several thorny violet colored weeds surrounded the bases of the dwarf trees, but not many other types of plants were visible. This most likely happened with good reason, for as the ice moved down the side of the mountain; cold edge of the ice sheets stripped away most vegetation in its path. Dead brown blades of grass covered most of the trail, and all were flattened pointed directly down hill, only their roots could have survived to try and flourish yet another year. I quickly learned that it was easier to follow the deer trail than it was to venture out on my own, for the brown blades that lay flattened, trapped droplets of water between them, making them difficult to stand on without them sliding out from under my feet.

As I made my way across the trail I passed over several areas laden with tiny sheets of ice and I found that even they were easier to negotiate than the areas of trampled grass.

As I neared the next peak, the sun had begun to set. It looked like I was going to have to sleep out in the open tonight, but by this point I didn't really care where I slept. Tired and hungry, I could now see the very top, only a hundred feet more to go. It had become a challenge for me, and by this point nothing else mattered. Across the short stretch of ground I continued on. When I was at the top, the achievement of this single-minded goal was all that really mattered. The lack of oxygen at this altitude coupled by the lack of food restricted me from thinking about anything else. I sat on the peak for over an hour. I was breathing heavier than usual and I needed more time to rest. I could see that mountains on all sides surrounded me, but I had to look for quite awhile before I became aware of this insight. The lighthearted feeble thinking feeling just would not pass. After briefly remembering that the sunset in the west, I calculated that the peaks that had the most snow were north of my position. Below me, was a valley that ran to the west towards more mountains and hills. I could see the reflection of the sun on the top of some water, and assumed that there was a river somewhere down there as well. Following what looked like a river westward, I saw what I was looking for.

"There it is," I could barely whisper with excitement. Down in the valley, some twenty miles away, was an area of light blue lights. It had to be a town. Without further hesitation, I clambered down the side of the mountain, but it was now dark, and without being able to see where I was going, I slipped on the grass and fell. This time the landing was not so soft, and I bruised my leg on a rock. I decided that I had better wait until daylight before I continued on. I went back up close to the top of the peak where I knew I could find shelter by several large outcroppings of rocks; I curled up in the fetal position, and promptly fell asleep.

Page 257

The sun rose early the next morning, but the clouds that had
accumulated during the night, kept the bright warm light from
shining down on me. I was in the middle of a deep sleep, and could
have slept longer if I had not been disturbed by an annoying noise.
A heavy thumping sound was coming from one of the lower
plateaus that I had ascended only the day before. I first heard the
noise as crashing thuds in the trees, but as I lay on the ground, I
could sense that the commotion was coming my way. I finally
decided that it was time to take a look, so I rose to my feet and felt
instantly dizzy as my blood rushed downward. I'm going to have to
take things easy at this higher altitude I reminded myself. From
where I stood I could see absolutely nothing, the clouds had moved
in and obscured the view of even the closest mountain. Only bits
and pieces of the river below showed through the misty clouds.
Hearing the noises once again reminded me of what had woken me
up in the first place. I wondered what in the world was going on? I
slowly walked over to the side of the peak. When I looked over
and down the side I couldn't believe my eyes because two plateaus
below me was the largest bear that I had ever seen. If he stood up
he would easily have been over twelve feet tall. His reddish-brown
fur was thick and ready for winter, which only added to his
oversized appearance. I was absolutely spellbound. The creature
was moving around rocks and eating what appeared to be hundreds
of moths. Hearing movements from up above, he quickly stood on
his two hind feet and surveyed the area. That was all the incentive I
needed to get my feet moving. After all, I was not about to feed the
bears, signs or no signs. The bear, however, was blocking the only
accessible trail that led down towards the river. At the other end of
the peak, twenty feet away, was a steep sloping cliff side filled
with brown flattened grass and patches of ice. I at first was hesitant
to climb down this way, but after contemplating being eaten alive
and at the sound of an ear-piercing growl, I jumped over the side. I
was now desperately trying to run down the side of the hill. I knew
that I could never outrun the bear, but if luck was on my side, I
could be gone before the bear saw or smelled me. Hearing me was

a whole other issue as the rocks moved out from beneath my feet. Soon I passed my first patch of ice and its accompanying pool of water and my feet became wet and slippery. Within seconds I was off balance and sliding down the hill. Not only was I traveling faster this way, but also I was using less energy, and in doing so, I could catch enough breath to grunt as my legs and buttocks took the main assault force of the downward sliding motion.

By the time the bear reached the top of the peak, I was half way down the deep slopping incline. So the bear just looked down at me. The hunt wasn't worth risking injuring a leg on this steep hill. I on the other hand, kept on going. I had cut my hands, ripped my pants, and was exhausted, but I kept going. When I finally had enough nerve to look back, there high on top of the peak sat the bear with his nose pointed towards me.

With the bears mouth shut, and lips smeared with moths, he gave the impression that he was smiling, or rather laughing at the badly bruised prey who had barely managed to elude him. Had the moths not been so plentiful, he would have followed after the lone human figure. Fortunately for the lone figure this was still early in spring and the slopes were just too slick with patches of ice around the bases of half frozen rocks to try something stupid like rushing down the side of the hill. It was best to use the trail and head down the hill towards the river where the berries were just ripening and the salmon would soon appear in the water. Food was plentiful, but the desire to kill the prey that had so often tried to hunt him, kept the image of the human in the back of his mind. Had he seen signs of a spear, he would have already moved away from the area.

I slid most of the way down. By now my body was bruised badly and my clothes were ripped to shreds, but I was still alive. Since the bear was smarter than me and obviously unwilling to follow me down this side of the hill, I decided to take a short break. During this short reprieve, all I could think of was how I was going to defend myself, but nothing in sight seemed of any defensive value. This side of the mountain was extremely different from the other side. There were no tall trees and a steady uphill grade separated by plateaus quite the opposite actually, just one long slope that started at the peak, and ended at the floor of the valley below. At a sixty-degree angle, the thought of having to continue down such a steep slope was unappealing, but being eaten alive sounded worse, so while I kept one eye out looking for the bear, I tried to determine the easiest way down. The slick brown grass was everywhere and there was nothing to hang on to except for an occasional dwarfed tree. Above me and below me I could see sheets of snow that were ready to tumble down into the valley with just the slightest suggestion of a vibration. I still would have preferred hiking back up to the top and going down the other side, had it not been for the bear. I was just about to consider circling the mountain below the bear and connecting back to the deer trail, but when I glanced up and found the beast to be no longer in sight, without further hesitation, I promptly headed straight down the slope, ripped pants and all.

By the time I reached the bottom of the mountain, only a few hours had passed. Quite a difference from the all day hike to ascend the day before, I thought, although I did have to thank the bear for the incentive to try a faster way down.

Sitting down to rest my feet, I gave one final look up towards the top. The monster was still nowhere in sight. I was glad because the flat footed moon boots had been hurting my feet so badly, that I doubted whether or not I could keep my feet moving any longer even if the bear was still following me.

After I had been sitting on the damp ground for a few minutes, I had no choice but to stand again. The ground was just too cold to rest on. Not only that, but going down the side of the mountain, the openings made by the tears in my pants had become entry points for cold damp air and the moisture was making my clothes wet. I was definitely going to have to reach town before the end of the day. Climbing over the rough terrain in moon boots would not be easy either. They were built specifically for the moon's gravitational field and not much else. As I was approaching the base of the mountain, I could clearly see the river's white churning waters and the banks full of greenery. Farther down and standing beside the underbrush, I could only hear the rushing roar of the river. Tall pine trees once again obscured the surrounding noises as well as the view. However, even without the pine trees, my range of vision would have still been limited by the low lying fog bank that out of nowhere moved in faster than I could have thought possible. It seemed to be the densest in the direction of where I had seen the lights of the town the night before. Even though I was sure that it was almost noon, because of the overhead position of the once unmistakable view of the sun, but the thick wedge of fog showed no signs of letting up and now I lost sight of my only source of warmth. This was to be the first in a series of sunless days that I was in no condition to deal with.

Walking beside the base of the mountain, I came to a large meadow. The meadow extended from the base of the mountain and led to the edge of the river. This had been the closest yet that I had been to the river. After the ordeal I had undergone the day before, I decided to avoid the underbrush as much as possible. This initially kept me away from the river, and also forced me to stay close to the base of the mountain. Not a bad decision after all, I thought as I proceeded to make my way across the meadow and neared the edge of the river. On the way across I could not help but notice the markings left behind by a large herd of deer.

Deer, elk, Caribou, they were all the same to me, and with little outdoor exposure to wildlife away from the seashore, there was little chance of me guessing correctly which species it was. I could only take note that the tracks were large and were hoof prints. The tracks led down to the bank of the river, and then they disappeared. Across, on the other side of the river, the tracks resumed up a short ridge. The water had to be cold as ice, I surmised, but that didn't seem to bother the herd that left the tracks. I would follow the trail down to the water, but there was no way that I was going to cross to the other side just to follow their well-groomed path through the underbrush. There had to be another way.

Then, suddenly, the smell of decaying flesh filled my nostrils, and thoughts of deer faded away. Skunk cabbage I assumed. I still had remnants of mud on me, but the smell of that had gone away. As I neared the edge of the embankment, the rancid smell increased ten fold. There was something that caught my eye as well. Bear tracks; they were everywhere. Then as I peered over the edge of the embankment I found out the reason why. There, no more than two feet below me was the remains of an old female elk. I wasn't sure if it was an elk, but it seemed much too big to be anything else. Most of the body had been torn apart, but the head was still intact, and that is all that I needed to base my judgment on. From the look of things, the carcass had not been there for more than a couple of days. Large paw prints stained the surrounding rocks red, leaving little mystery as to what had happened. I now knew why the bear had not cared to chase me. He had eaten too much to bother with me. Then I remembered my own hunger. So after a quick pause, I walked down the embankment and headed along the shoreline towards the town.

I continued walking beside the river for most of the day and not once did the sun break through the clouds for more than a minute. On the way, I stopped several times to eat berries that I spotted, but this didn't really help much. What I needed was some fast food like a burger and fries, or even a pastrami sandwich. While my stomach growled, I thought about all of the various types of sandwiches that I would like to have right now. I didn't even try to ignore the feelings of hunger, I was too certain that the town was close at hand and I would have access to white bread and mayonnaise any minute now.

As I neared the area where I had seen the light the night before, my opinion as to how far away the location was changed. I should have already come across signs of other people I thought to myself. Unfortunately, all I had seen so far were the forest creatures. I also would have to cross a bridge to get to the other side of the river, they must have a bridge to cross over to hunt here, but I could see none. So now the question was, just how isolated was this town from the rest of the world? As I continued on, I began to doubt that I had even seen the glow of a city's night-lights. After all, the only time I had seen it, was when I was on top of the peak and suffering from hypoxia. This thought did nothing to reassure me, and with the low-lying fog covering my view. There was no other way to prove that I had been correct. I would just have to press on and discover what I could.

More time had passed, and I knew that I was no more than five miles away from where I had seen the town lights. The only problem was that I still believed that I had to cross the river to get there. I reached down to touch the water, thinking that I just might have to swim.

"Oh no!..." I rapidly withdrew my frozen blue hand from the river. The water was ice cold, and the dirty brown color did not make it too appealing to drink either. I decided that the best thing that I could do now was to sit down and try and come up with a plan. I began tossing small stones into the water while I looked over to the other side. The fog still shrouded the valley, but it was slowly burning off. Less than half a mile away downstream, the river was narrower. The water was smooth with no visible currents, but a raft would have taken a week to build, and there was no way that I was going to swim across on my own, so I decided to spend the night here. Maybe in the morning the fog would completely lift and someone would spot me from the air, I hoped. I preoccupied myself by watching the sunset, dark red and orange streaks painted the sky, while the sun glowed a bright luminescent golden orange. I reflected back to my visit on the moon. I really missed all of this, and although I was tired, lost, and hungry, it felt good to be back on Earth. As darkness descended, sleep claimed my body and mind.

That night the fog lifted, but fog had given way to rain and time and time again, the rain poured down upon me. By the time the sun was rising, the moonsuit was drenched, as well as my own under clothes. I had been awakened several times as I tried to keep warm, but even after moving under a tall tree, I still fought a losing battle to stay warm and dry. When the rain finally ceased, three Canadian geese flew overhead signaling that it was going to be a very good day. Sure enough, as I left the protection of the tree branches and looked up, I could see an almost cloudless sky. A large smile filled my face, but quickly faded as I turned in the direction of the town. I was absolutely stunned. For what appeared to be the soft blue lights of a town, was nothing more than a massive glacier. This was the first time that I had ever seen a glacier in real life, but I was sure that this is what it had to be. Even from across the river I could see the unmistakable signs of a few large crevasses that broke into smaller ones as they worked their way from the top, where the ice was light blue, down to the foot of the glacier where the ice turned dingy gray. The view was spectacular, but was over shadowed as my stomach began to growl and a surge of rage overtook me.

"Where on Earth am I?" I shouted with fists clenched and raised in the air and with eyes squinting from the glaring sun. I wasn't sent to help humanity; I've been abandoned. They left me to die where no other man could find me. I slumped back to the ground. I had never been a quitter, and this time was no exception.

I was going to survive, but for what or why, were the questions disturbing me now.

"I will get revenge!" Screaming out released some of my frustrations, but utilized a great deal of energy, energy that I could ill-afford to waste. The lack of a decent meal had been taking its toll on me, but until this recent burst of emotion, I could tolerate my condition. Now, however, I was spent. I had to find something other than berries to eat, or I wouldn't make it to town. The problem was what? There was no way I could drag down one of those deer, even if I could get close enough. The only natural thing for me to do now was to follow the river and try to find something to eat along the way, maybe a fish perhaps. At this point even the prospect of finding a half dead fish sounded good, but luck was on my side and soon after walking I came upon something more appealing.

There, near the edge of the water, was one of the geese that I had seen fly overhead earlier. The goose seemed to be resting for the long flight ahead. Shoving its face underwater, from time to time to quench its thirst, the bird seemed quite content to just relax and bask in what sun was available. I told myself that I had to get this bird.

Quickly looking around, I grabbed a piece of driftwood and carefully approached the bird. The goose at first appeared to pay no attention to my figure, but when it began to show signs of agitation, I stopped and froze in place. All my efforts depended on a swift and precise attack. The goose by this point was looking directly at me and was shifting its agitated weight from side to side. If I came any closer, my fear was that the bird would flee into the air. I was standing over thirty feet away. I had to get closer, but I couldn't take the chance of him taking off. The only thing to do was to stand perfectly still and hope that the bird would move closer to me. I stood for several moments as I watched for the right opportunity. The bird had to weigh over twenty pounds, but even as big as it was, from where I was standing, the head was almost too small of a target to aim at. The most I could hope for was to hit it and in doing so, cripple it badly enough so that it couldn't fly and I could try and catch it. The plan was simple, but relied heavily on my ability to throw a wet half rotted stick accurately. After a short window of opportunity I thought I would lose the bird, for overhead, I spotted a familiar movement. Looking up, I immediately recognized the outline of an eagle.

"Looks like I have competition," I quietly said to myself. The goose saw the eagle a split second even before I did and began to panic. It was now or never I thought. The goose seemed to sense my intentions, and with the first sign of movement, it took off. I came running having already thrown the piece of wood. The goose easily raised its body out of the way of the ensuing piece of wood as it clamored for more height. I still ran for a now imaginary spot and then turned my neck to watch the goose rise up over the river. Then suddenly, before I could fathom what was happening, the eagle gripped on to the right wing of the goose. The two of them began to swirl in an upward direction as the goose frantically tried to free itself from the eagle's clutches. It was one of the most fantastic sights that I had ever witnessed. I was sure that the eagle had won the battle, but as quickly as the battle began, the two separated. Somehow, the eagle was caught off guard and lost its vice-like grip. In bewilderment, it glided in a large arc to see what had happened.

In the meantime, the goose plummeted downward. Something was wrong; the right wing was deeply injured and would not function properly. The left wing flapped through the air, but could not sustain the entire weight of the bird. Down the goose came with the eagle closing in for a second try, but the eagle was too late. Carried by its own momentum, the goose hit the river like a rock. Immediately its movements ceased. The spot where it had fallen was less than twenty feet away from the shore in a swirling backwater eddy. I could almost taste the goose from where I was standing. I knew now that I would have to act quickly, for the eagle after not returning in time for the second air attack, was sure to circle around to snatch the dead bird out of the water. The thought of the eagle stealing the bird first was too much to bear. I found myself diving into the water after the goose. The eagle noted my approach and veered away. Not being familiar with the large figure like me was reason enough to take precautions. Veering away would cost him his meal, but food was abundant and soon he would be swooping down with his talons on another unwary prey.

Adrenaline was filling my body. I was so intent on reaching the goose that I did not even see the eagle climb up over the mountain peaks. I was almost delirious by the time I reached the goose. When I did, I grabbed it as if it was still able to escape. The limp neck bobbed under the water several times before I was fully aware that I had won the prize.

My teeth were chattering, but I still yelled out victoriously "I got it," but only said it once as I was starting to feel overwhelmed by hypothermia. The full effect of the cold water inundated my senses. The thought of freezing to death began to down play my victorious feat. I held on to the Goose's neck as if my hand was frozen, which it was. Get back to shore, a message flashed in my brain and then repeatedly sent the signal to the rest of my body. Soon the message broke through to my numbed muscles, and I responded by turning around to face the shore. Looking back, all I could do was gasp. I hadn't noticed it, but there was a current in the river. One that was strong enough to put me in the middle of the river in less than half a second. I realized that my reactions had slowed some, but I never would have predicted such a displacement in so short a time. Swimming back would now be one of the most difficult problems to face so far, but as I tried, I found it quite impossible. The movement of the river on that side was too fast and tended to push towards the other bank. As my swimming pace slowed with fatigue, I found myself closer to the opposite shore, so I eventually gained enough clarity and aimed his sights on reaching that shore instead. It had been the wisest choice, for up ahead, as I neared the embankment, I could see a gray colored river merging with the one I was already in. Choking and sputtering out water, I crawled up onto a two-foot tall, sloping embankment with the goose still secure in my death-like grip. When I was out of the water, I dropped the goose on the ground stripped off my wet moonsuit and undergarments and passed out from exhaustion.

PAGE 271

I woke up as the sun rose overhead. I had no idea how long I was
out all I knew was that I was laying on the ground with something
covering my body. A foot away from my nose was half a salmon.
There were ants on it tearing away microscopic pieces then
carrying the flesh away, yet the salmon still smelled better than any
sushi that I ever had the pleasure of devouring. I was definitely
starving. I tried to reach over to the salmon and a pile of grass, dirt,
and a rock fell off my arm. I was covered with twigs, branches,
moss, dirt, and a more rocks half the size of my head. I was lying
were I fell over and passed out, but someone or something had
covered my body as if to bury me alive. And as if this wasn't bad
enough, my goose was gone. I rose to my feet and brushed as
much dirt and debris off my body as I could. I looked at the ground
all around me and my goose was definitely missing, but in its place
I had been given a whole side of salmon. A small fire pit told me
that whoever had been here had spent some time next to me and
that's when I noticed the blacked smudges on the rocks that fell off
me as I rose to my feet. Someone was playing a trick on me, but
my clothes were right where I flung them off my body. As I picked
the still wet garments up that I would have died from hypothermia
had I still been wearing them, that's when it hit me, all that dirt and
debris including the aid of formerly headed rocks purposely set on
my body had helped conserve my core body temperature. Had I
been left uncovered, I might have died from exposure. Someone
had heated the rocks to help me stay warm. Someone had in effect
saved my life. I was also left alive with half a raw salmon split
down the middle as apposed to dead with an uncooked goose. I
would have to thank them if I ever saw them. In the meantime I
hung my clothes on nearby branches and ate some raw salmon
while I waited for the noonday sun to come out and dry my
clothes.

     Working through the densely packed foliage caused me to
perspire heavily. With my clothes a little more than half dry I was
on the move again. As I stepped past the last tenacious tree in my
way, a cold wind whipped across my face and froze the beads of
sweat in place. Out of response, I rubbed my forearm against my

face and instantly felt warmer. In front of me, only two hundred feet away, was the glacier. The wind that had tried to freeze me was coming straight off the top of glacier and down onto the lake. The view here was worth the effort I decided. I looked at the dirty pebble riddled foot of the glacier then directed my gaze towards the top bowl area. The ice turned to shades of light blue and white and was more pure and colorful than anything I had ever seen above water. Swept up by the natural beauty, I decided to attempt to climb on the glacier to see what more hidden beauty lay ahead. I looked for a way to climb the foot of the glacier, but quickly concluded that it wasn't going to be easy. The base of the glacier was continuously breaking up at various points as it melted away under the guidance of the sun's rays. Some of the most obtrusive sections had air gaps between earth and ice that raised four feet off the ground before forming a randomly slanted ten-foot high leading edge. The leading edge of ice refracted the sun's rays like one massively long, one-foot thick diamond. A small stream of water ran down hill on the substrate beneath the raised up portions of ice and returned underground where chunks of ice had broken away from the main body of the glacier. Not far from where I was standing, a large piece of granite formed a rock wall to halt the onslaught of the glacier. It was here that I would have the best chance of finding a way to climb onto the ice. So around a small standing lake of water I strode, and up the face of the rock I began climbing. Standing on the top of the rock, I was thirty feet above the lake, and twenty feet above the base of the glacier. Directly in front of me stood a twelve-foot long slope that almost met flush against the rock. Some of the ice was very thin, did not rub next to rock, and was transparent. I could look between the crack and see the small stream of water flowing beneath the ice. While I debated whether this area was safe enough to cross over, I saw to my right another rocky structure that appeared to be fused together with the foot of the glacier. After taking one more glance down at the steam, I decided to try another spot. I traversed a rock filled marsh area, and up the next ridge. This place was definitely safer I decided. Here the ice was deep white and frozen solid; not even a glimmer of looking weak. I leisurely walked down a mere four feet and onto the glacier. The feeling of being on an actual glacier was exulting, but my feet kept trying to slip out from under me. I took each step ever so slowly so I wouldn't risk falling on the rock hard surface. After I had crossed a good distance onto the glacier, I stopped to look around. Ahead of me the sheet of ice curved upward. There would be no way for me to maintain my traction unless I stayed on the leveled out areas. Even the slightest amount of uneven ice was all it took to making my out of place and overly worn and torn pair of moon boots begin to give ground and let me slip and slide. Surveying my surroundings I tried to judge a logical way to gradually ascend up the light blue mountain of ice.

Taking my time, I had made it up and over some sixty feet. In front of me was the top over a mile away and another two thousand feet higher in elevation. There is no way to go any further, I admitted to myself. To the right was a tall sloping wall of the edge of a crevasse. At the base of the wall was a deep dark blue hole through which a small trickle of water poured. The trickle ran down a foot or less, then went back under the ice. The ice around the base was transparent and allowed me to see a few feet through it. Only a few feet from the base of the hole, was a circle of deep blue surrounded by deep white.

Carefully, I edged over to the hole and held my outstretched hand under the trickle of water. It was as cold as the surrounding ice, but I found the taste to be extraordinarily refreshing. It had been a long time since I had sampled water like this. The water in Fiji always tasted like the coral wells that it came from unless it was the bottled brand that was filtered. As far as I was concerned, most water supplies tasted like "chemical city", but this water was pure. I wish I could take back the recipe for this I thought to myself. Having filled my stomach with thousand year old glacier water, I turned to look back at the lake down at the base of the glacier. I could sit here for hours, watching ice gradually melt and birds chase one another and dive in the clearness of the sky and water. Keeping my eye on the birds, I watched as they returned over and over again with food to their nests. Below and not too far away, a group of black and white colored terns huddled over their eggs. Far to the right, a hodgepodge of smaller aviators fought over other nesting sites. I, for a brief moment, felt content in this strange new environment. I always found a source of wonder and delight in the marvels of nature. While looking at the tern nests to see which was the easiest to reach, something totally out of place caught my attention. Over by a large grouping of rocks were the remnants of a well worn-out fire pit. The pit was charcoal black, along with the sides of the surrounding boulders. The grass nearby was composed of different shades of brown and black, but what struck me the most was a small plume of smoke signifying that a fire was still alive. This meant that there had to be someone close by. A mountain climber, hunter, or backpacker I excitedly thought. I cupped my hands to my mouth and shouted with all my strength, "hello". My voice seemed to be muffled by the ice, but I was sure that if anyone were near, they would at least hear something.

"Hello," I bellowed again. A brown pile of fur moved to look my way. It had been setting next to the fire, but half-hidden by blending in with the shade of the rocks. A face peered out from under the huge piece of brown fuzzy hide, but from where I was standing, I couldn't see more than someone I didn't recognize wearing a short black beard.

"Hello down there." I was rewarded with silence. The face only stared back at me. Having become excited by finally finding someone, I tried to race down the glacier as quickly as I could. This proved to be a bad decision, for I promptly fell, landing on my posterior, and I began what was to be the fastest way down that in my right mind, I could never have possibly chosen. I desperately tried to stop, but it proved to be an impossible feat. The ice tossed me around like a bowling ball shooting down a crooked gutter. My body was turned and swiveled up one ridge and down another, yet I only seemed to gain momentum. My perception of the first second of my journey lasted over three minutes, the next two seconds lasted a lifetime. Screaming at the top of my lungs, I watched helplessly as my body sailed into the air. For a moment I was suspended over a large crevasse, the interior a deep iridescent blue, and bottomless. A heavy landing on the other side was my indication that I had escaped the treacherous death trap. Unfortunately, the velocity of my sliding body hadn't seemed to diminish, and the edge of glacier was fast approaching like a finish line except that this one ended with a twenty-foot drop. I could see that I was heading in the direction of the campfire. Only a small mound of Earth had to be crossed to reach the spot, but as I neared the drop off, I felt panic rising up in my throat. The foot of the ice was at least fifteen feet above terra firma, a soft landing would not be in store for me, it would be like falling shirtless and without a helmet off a Harley motorcycle on a gravel road while going full speed, and I started counting the number of broken bones I would soon receive.

By now I was facing down hill similar in the position superman was portrayed flying and across the edge I indeed flew. Looking ahead I saw my projection path was aiming me for a small puddle of water. In that split second I wondered if I would skip like a rock before I split in two. The birds surrounding the water quickly took off as the incoming object, me, came rolling closer. Suddenly, the journey was over. I had missed the potential soft landing in the water by a few inches. Instead, I had landed in the gravel as I first predicted. The momentum pushed my head into the dirt, and I suddenly had to fight to breath. Turning over to my side, I coughed, choked, and spit out small pieces of rock.

"I think I'm in one piece," I concluded as I rolled on my back and just lay on the ground, although I couldn't shake the dizzy spinning feeling out of my head. While my mind cleared, my nose was beginning to burn and swell. Bringing my fingers up to explore the damage sent waves of pain radiating throughout face.

"Thank you," I muttered in a high muffled nasal tone. I just realized that I had broken my nose. I ever so carefully touched my face, and found my nose slanted towards the left. Very carefully I brought both of my hands together and quickly jerked my nose back to its normal position. Instantaneously the pain soared around my nose and I yelped in agony. At this point, I wished that it had been my leg or arm that had broken. My entire face raged with hurt, and I had one of the worst headaches ever, trying to rip apart my head. Trying to raise my head while wiping blood off my chin, I decided right then to give up the beauty and splendor of glacier hiking. It was definitely safer swimming with poisonous sea snakes.

Feeling not near well enough to stand upright, I rose up best as I could and staggered across a small mound of rubble towards where I thought the campfire should be located. Although the wind whipped at my back as I moved, it died once I descended over the other side of the mound. This must be one of the reasons why this spot was selected for the campsite. Only a short distance away I could see two brown eyes peering out from the huddled mass beneath the animal skin. The fur was covered with soil and was matted from constant use. It was also primitively sewn together in sections with thick strips of leather, but it looked warm compared to what I was wearing. I couldn't figure out what type of creature the fur once belonged to, but I could definitely think of better ways for a homeless person to stay warm; namely Gore-Tex outer material and polyester layering.

As I looked closer, I noticed the figure huddled under the blanket, I think it was a man, was holding the side of his jaw and he had a strange look of fear and pain mixed in his eyes. He had seen me fly down from the ice. He had heard me moaning in pain on the other side of the mound, and now I was standing like a bloody mess in front of him. As far as he knew, I had come to attack him, steal what little possessions he owned, and that his death was imminent.

As I approached him, I saw the man curl up tightly into what could only be the fetal position. The man obviously had been out here for a long time, for his face was covered with dirt and hair. He had some broken tree branches next to the fire that was dying out, yet he made no attempt to move and I stoked the fire with more wood. I moved over towards the branches and place some of them on the smoldering fire coals. They smoked for a second then flames began to take them. The man tried to curl tighter, and in doing so the fur moved away from his face and revealed his whole hand tightly pressed against the left side of his face. The man appeared to be injured, and was moaning in pain. My presence only seemed to exacerbate the man's intolerable condition. Standing over him, I reached down and pulled the fur off his head and exposing his shoulders and chest. The man did little to resist me other that bringing his other hand up to cover his first hand. It was then that I got a clear view of his face and I felt my own mind being shocked back into awareness, for here, lying at my feet, was a man that could have come from the pages of a history book. His extended jaw line, low elongated sloping head, and large protruding eye brow ridge were definite deformities, and the rest of his extremely strong muscled, yet hairy body resembled Neanderthals that I had so often seen depicted as standing wax figures in museums, pumping iron at sports gyms, and occasionally

shopping at Walmart. No wonder he was out here in the
wilderness, he had probably found it more pleasant to be alone
with nature than being shunned or made fun of by his fellow
humans.

He really looked weird I thought, but the wavering eyes
before me were full of pain and somehow I felt those eyes were
pleading for help. It then dawned on me what the problem was,
from the position of his hands and the swollen outline of the left
side of his face; I could sense that he had been here for several
days, probably without anything to eat, and all because of a bad
tooth.

"Let me see," I commanded as I kneeled down in front of
him. The man did not acknowledge my words, but he remained
perfectly still. It was as if the man had already accepted death. I
pulled the man's hands away, revealing a red swollen jaw. The area
inside his mouth must have been infected for quite some time, for
even the surrounding outer layer of facial hair had begun falling
away; a natural reaction when surrounding tissues were damaged.
Upon opening his mouth, a powerful foul odor filled the air.
Fortunately, the damage done to my nose made me mostly breath
through my mouth, ironically keeping me from becoming
nauseated. The inside of the man's gums were bleeding, especially
around the left lower canine, the tooth itself, was oddly discolored
and slightly elongated.

"Boy, what my Dentist would give to see your teeth." I
peered around the man's mouth. All the other man could do was
hold his head back with his mouth open and hope that death would
come swift and quickly release him from his pain.

"What I think you need is a root canal, but you could die
from infection before you ever make it to a Dentist. Now, I think I
can pull it out for you, but it's going to hurt." I sat back on my
haunches and studied the man. I realized how ridiculous I sounded.
The man was going to die from a simple tooth infection. The
whole situation seemed dumbfounding. Why the man didn't
remove it himself, just like actors did in countless movies, I would
never know. I was going to have to do it for him. I wasn't going to
let the only other human that I had encountered, die and leave me
alone no matter what he looked or smelled like. Tearing some cloth
off of my undershirt, I carefully inserted it into the man's mouth.

Bringing the cloth around the dead tooth, I gripped the cloth tightly.

"This is going to hurt, but it will soon be over," the words were for my own reassurance, if nothing else. With a quick forceful pull, I jerked down and outward on the cloth with all my might. The man tried to scream in pain, but could only spit out the ensuing blood as he clamped his lips together. I fell backwards with the cloth still tightly gripped in my hand. Embedded in the fabric was the literal roots and tooth of the man's problems. The elongated tooth was unlike any other human tooth that I had ever seen before. I sat on the nearby grass, proud of his accomplishment; I stoked the fire while my new Neanderthal like friend rolled inside his fur covering while moaning in pain. Several times he spit out blood and other fluids before the pain began to subside. Finally, he became silent as if he died although most likely he had just fallen asleep. Probably, this was the first good sleep that he had had in days.

In the meantime, I added more wood to the fire. I then sat back and looked at the sleeping figure. Before now, I didn't have any free time to contemplate my present reality. The man was close to death, and I had to rectify that situation above all else. Now, however, as I scrutinized the prehistoric outline of my one and only new friend, an ill-at-ease feeling over whelmed me. Could I have been sent back in time farther than I had originally assumed? I could only hope that the man in front of me was the byproduct of bad genes and a living outcast from modern civilization. The other alternative I didn't want to think about. After all, why was I sent here? What could I do to help out the human race at such a time when the race was just barely two legs up over other primates?

"You are a mutant, aren't you?" The sleeping form didn't budge. "I hope with all my soul you are, or I'm in a whole lot of trouble." I held the tooth up to look at it again. Then, after a while, turning back to the fire, I stared into the flames until I too fell asleep.

PAGE 281

In the morning I woke to the smell of burning hair. Lying on the frigid ground, I rose up and rubbed the smoke out of my eyes. Accidentally my hands brushed against my nose, and I immediately remembered what had happened the day before. With my eyes freed from bits of ashes, I could see a rabbit skewered on a stick and being pressed against the flames by my newly found friend. Looking at the man's face, I could see that some of the swelling of his jaw had receded. Glancing back at the rabbit, I began to chuckle, which in turn, led to all out laughter. Here was a primitive man cooking over a fire, while I myself, a modern man, was reduced to raw food just the day before. It was obvious that the word primitive, in this case, had been associated with the wrong man. My friend noticed me laughing, and tried to join in, but that only seemed to make his jaw hurt worse. The pain showed in his face and I quickly stopped, got up and walked over to him.

"Open your mouth and let's have a look." The man stood still while I took my hands and opened his mouth and looked inside.

"It's definitely improving," I said for no apparent reason. The lower gum line, as well as the hole where the tooth formerly resided had stopped bleeding. Much of the swelling had decreased and the general outline of his mouth resumed a more normal appearance. I searched on the ground for the tooth. Upon finding the elongated structure, I held it up in front of my new friend.

"This tooth is bad. However, I know a man in Fiji who would give you just about anything to wear it on his necklace." The man stared at me quizzically, but remained silent. It was like talking to a wall, I thought, but at least I was not physically alone and besides, I had also found myself a good cook or at least someone who could snare rabbits.

When the rabbit had browned and with the meat slightly separating from the bone, the man passed it to me. I broke off a large hind leg, and then returned it to my new friend, who in turn tore off several large strips. I watched as he tried to manipulate the

168

meat in his injured mouth. I was still wondering how the man could have captured the rabbit, given his present condition. In the meantime, the man watched as I ate the piece he offered me. He studied my broken nose and the fact that my skin was mostly hairless except to fine hair on my arm. He looked over at the edge of the glacier and back at me then over at the glacier again. He did this several times as if he was trying to figure out how I could fly. He out weighed me by at least fifty pounds and I think it was my thin build that helped me sail so far before plummeting to Earth.

He noticed that I wasn't eating so he motioned for me to eat with his hands. He also let out a slight grunt as if he would have spoken had it not been for his sore mouth. After so little food, the rabbit tasted heavenly compared to the sashimi dish of yesterday. I wouldn't put it in the same class as Church's fried chicken, but I easily devoured half of it. After finishing, I decided to stretch my legs by walking over to the edge of the small lake.

"Well what now," I murmured to myself as I peered into the water. The sound of another pair of footsteps startled me. I turned around to see my large eye browed friend patiently standing not far behind me. He was dressed in his fur garment and clutching to the remains of his share of rabbit in his right hand, a long heavy spear was clutched in the other.

"That reminds me, I wonder what happened to my spear?" I looked up on the glacier, but could not see it. My friend also looked at the glacier, but wondered if that was where we soon would be going. I noticed that the primitive man's spear was over seven feet long and two inches thick. At the end there was a sharp well-shaped flint point tied to the wooden shaft and held firmly in place by some sort of black ash colored resin. Next to this, my former spear was nothing but a puny stick that could barely be used for drawing faces in the sand. Although the man was only around five feet tall, his muscles and body structure looked stronger than my own. Even though the man was in a weakened condition, he was a regular compact yet formidable tank. I could never have the muscular power he did even if I worked out every day at the gym. I didn't even want to contemplate what my friend thought of me, but a few unbidden thoughts crossed my mind: tall, skinny, and not much muscle. However, he seemed to be waiting as if I was in charge.

"I definitely need to make another spear," I stated and walked over to the edge of a wooded grove with my friend moving right behind me. I was nearly a third of the way around the small lake, and I wasn't going any further, I knew that the bear might still be hanging around somewhere close by. After I selected an appropriate sized branch, one that was only six feet long, I pulled out my knife and began to whittle the end of the stick into a point. My friend watched in amazement. First he was awe struck at the shinny silver blade, and then how I was able to condense an hour's worth of work using sharp edged stones into a few minutes worth of time. I think he was grateful I didn't use the shiny object to take out his tooth.

"That'll do nicely!" I tested the pointed end with my finger. "It doesn't have the fine flint point like yours, but at least now I can defend myself." I closed my knife and returned it to my side pocket. Examining what was left of my moon exploration suit, I came to the conclusion that I would probably be dressing like my friend sooner than I expected. The moon suit material was deteriorating rapidly; there were several tears and well-worn spots at the elbows and knees. I felt my friend's hand touch the pocket of my suit where I had inserted my knife.

"Whoa, there," I yelled out. He stopped and just looked at me and grinned.

"I suppose this does look a little out of the ordinary to you, but don't worry, I'm afraid that I'll be dressed just like you in a couple of weeks. That is if it takes me that long to find my way out of here." As an afterthought, I decided that the Neanderthal was dressed rather well for this type of climate. Two long pieces of fur sewn together by large threads flowed down to his knees and were held tight around his waist by a narrow cord of fur. His legs were covered by wraps of fur that went all the way down to his feet, resembling long boots, again bound tightly against his skin by strands of leather and fur. His head was covered with long dark hair that only left his eyes, mouth, and the large scar on his nose exposed. This was certainly enough to keep his head warm. Even if I had years to waste here, I still doubted that I could ever accumulate that much hair on my face. I would just have to let the wind blow and cover up when times were rough. Realizing that my friend was becoming nervous by my uncomfortable visual examination, I quickly decided to overt my attention.

"Which way do we go to get out of here?" I pointed in several directions, but my companion gave me a blank expression, then pointed towards the glacier. I shook my head.

"No. I'm not going to try that trick again. Show me another way." My friend didn't understand a single word, but he was sure that I was against going towards the glacier, at least for the moment. Both of us stood in silence for several minutes. We had come to an impasse, and we were getting nowhere and I had the feeling he could wait twice as long as I could.

"Now look, I'm lost, and I know you don't understand me, but you have to lead the way, and I have to follow." The words floated in the air, but did not provoke any response from my friend. It was as if he was afraid to talk in front of me. Perhaps he thought that if I didn't like what he had to say, only bad omens could come from it, and I would take out another tooth.

He was looking at me as if I was in the middle of telling a hunting story, he couldn't understand the words, but the actions were clear. First the spear, then the pointing in all directions, what else could it mean, he reasoned. The Neanderthal watched as I finally became silent, and sat down on a rock that rose above the frozen tundra. Only a walking spirit would sit so exposed for all predators to see without a care in the world, he thought. He stood silently waiting for the spirit's next movements but there were none.

I peered out onto the small lake trying to figure a way for us to communicate, but the task appeared hopeless. My new friend had not uttered a word since we met and there was little evidence that he would in the future.

The man tried to see what the spirit was looking at in the lake, but could see nothing. Maybe spirits saw more than he, he would never know. After an hour had passed, he was still standing; the spirit was still sitting in the same spot with his eyes still piercing through the lake. It was then that his attention was distracted from the spirit to a familiar repugnant smell and ominous sound coming closer from the nearby-forested area. Instinctively he took several steps backward as the sound resonated closer.

"Well it's about time you moved," I sarcastically remarked. I then saw the uncertain look on my friend's face just as the primitive man turned around and began walking quickly towards the foot of the glacier.

"I told you that I'm not going that way." But the primitive man broke out in a full run, clutching to both his spear and rabbit fur. I could think of nothing else to do but follow. The strides of my long legs, quickly let me catch up to my friend, but I did not have the stamina to remain with him for very long. Soon, I was slowing down, my friend never looked back once. Finally I stopped and watched my friend climb up onto a tall boulder, and throw him self on top of the foot of the glacier. He landed almost flat and remained there motionless. I thought that he was absolutely mad, but a loud crackling noise from the edge of a small group of trees dispelled any notion that my friend was crazy. For there, breaking off the lower lying limbs of the tree, was the largest elephant that I had ever seen. This was no ordinary elephant, but a woolly mammoth. I starred in awe as he rubbed his tusks against the sides of the trees. He was marking the territory with his scent. Perhaps he was in musk, a heightened state of hormones and ready to mate. As I watched the power that was used in such an instinctive and yet uncontrollable way, I dropped my newly made spear and reached down for my knife and opened the blade. Then suddenly two things happened, one was that I remembered reading about rogue elephants, and the other was that the elephant took notice of the tiny human figure that was me. The beast snorted and grunted one last time at the trees, and immediately began a full charge towards me. I knew that a rogue elephant would try to kill anything in its vicinity, and by the looks of this reaction, he was not going to make any exception for me. With this simple summation, a burst of adrenaline shot through my body and I followed my friend's lead. Still some twenty feet from the boulder my friend used to leap up onto the ice, I could hear the movements of the beast bearing down on me. I quickly began to doubt whether or not I would make it up the boulder and onto the ice in time. The negative consequences of that thought, gave me further waves of adrenaline, and so I shot even further ahead. Ten feet from the boulder, the moon boots were killing my feet and I vowed to take them off the moment I reached safety. Now I could hear each breath that the large bulky mass behind drew and expelled. The air around me smelled like half digested grass. The wind was blowing towards me at a very fast pace. There was no time to look back. I was only seconds from the base of the glacier. Reaching the boulder, I jumped up into the air, took two steps up the side of the boulder, and sailed upward towards the top of the ice. My friend witnessed the movement, and was sure that I had flown.

I was momentarily suspended in mid-air. Behind me I heard a terrible roar, followed by a large thumping noise. I was only a fraction of a second away from landing on an area of ice that was beginning to move. This was because the mammoth had run his body into the foot of the glacier. As I landed, the angle of the ice shifted and cracked beneath me. It was a hard landing. I could feel sharp shooting pains in my chest and nose. Realizing that my body was sliding down towards the edge of the ice, I gripped my hands on my knife and jabbed deeply against the ice. Eventually the tip of the knife sunk into a soft spot, and my body abruptly halted its downhill movement. I would now have to remain frozen and hope that the patch of ice that I was on would not move again. I was facing uphill, out of harms way, but my feet were very close to the edge of the ice. My friend sat in astonishment as he watched the mammoth place his front feet on top of the boulder and try to pursue his enemies. A normal mastodon would have stayed completely clear of this area of ice. For they instinctively knew that the ice could not hold their weight if it was hued a particular color. They would normally refrain from such areas, but this one had gone mad. As my primitive friend watched, the mammoth reached out over the ice, and tried swinging his tusks at the spirit man in order to knock him off the ice.

I felt something hard hit against my ankle, but it didn't cause me any real pain, but I could not get a clear view of what caused it. Looking down at the ice, wondering what to do, I noticed that my nose had begun to bleed again. My friend saw the blood, and then looked at my nose. A chill of fear suddenly swept through his body, for once again the nose was colored red. He knew that the mammoth had caused the spirit to become angry, but he still felt that he would be the one to receive the spirit's wrath. He lay in terror as he watched the beast try to reach me. Several times the animal swayed his body and raked his tusks back and forth across the ice, each time trying to connect them with the legs of my helpless figure. The mammoth's head was a massive sight to behold, and the primitive man trembled as he watched the shaggy beast's tusks finally make contact with my body and try and nock me off the ice. I felt a wave of pain as a lengthy piece of ivory slammed into the side of my body, and I slid closer to the edge of the ice.

Suddenly, as the beast tried to lift my body, my primate friend could stand it no more. Swiftly he rose to his feet and charged at the massive mastodon. Stealthily aiming his spear, he threw it at the small left eye. The spear landed with deadly accuracy and he rushed forward to drive it farther into the eye socket and deeper inside the brain case with the might of his bare hands. The mammoth tried to back down off the boulder, suspending my friend in the air in the process. Blood began spewing out of the wound, and the stricken animal let out a series of hideous screams. I could not believe the strength and courage that my friend possessed. Tumbling to the ground, the beast caused the earth to shake, as well as the surrounding foot of the glacier. Some of the ice broke free from the main body, while other pieces slightly tilted and became unstable. In the end, there was enough movement to wrench the tip of my knife out of the ice and I abruptly felt my body begin to slide. Over the edge I tumbled, but this time my landing was soft. Feeling the heavy movements beneath me, I carefully crawled off the woolly brown body and looked at the massive outline of the mammoth. This is no dream I told myself. I was back in time, and I was almost killed by a creature that died out at least ten thousand years ago.

As I looked at the hole that the spear had made, I suddenly remembered the man who saved me. Turning in a quick half circle, I spotted him lying still on the ground with his hand still clenched tightly around the piece of rabbit fur. He must have been knocked unconscious. I glanced back at the beast; it was in its final moments of life, the chest raising less with each breath. A wheezing noise emanated from its trunk with a trickle of blood pooling around its head. My friend must have hit an artery. I felt saddened, I had a lot of respect for the fallen adversary, and I knelt down next to the beast and stroked the coarse fur.

"Soon there will be no more of your kind." As the animal took its last deep breath, the wheezing ceased, I searched for a heartbeat, but it was a futile attempt; there was none. Only an erratic series of muscle contractions kept me from pronouncing him dead. Standing up, I noticed a small stream of water coming off the glacier close by and decided to make my way over to it. There was simply too much to deal with, and the thought of cool water sounded like salvation. Bending over the stream, I splashed the frigid water onto my face. The water numbed my nose and I felt instant relief. Looking over at the two figures lying on the ground, I shook my head and returned to the sweet cold succor the stream offered. I once again splashed water on my face and then looked in the direction of the two fallen creatures. Neither had moved.

"This is not a dream, I must face reality." I rubbed my forehead as if to help my brain absorb what just transpired. I finally concluded that tending to my friend's needs would be my next best move. So I took off a moon boot and filled it with water.

Standing over the fallen figure, I let the water droplets flow from the boot and land on my friend's face. My friend immediately began to awaken with a rather annoyed look on his face. I was glad to see that he was all right, but at the same, my friend's facial features also concerned me. Having mammoths ruling the environment proved that I was indeed back in time, but the features of this non-deformed Neanderthal only worsened my fears that I was back farther in time than I dared contemplate.

"Well I'm glad to see that you're alright." I watched as the man rose to his feet. No bones appeared to be broken. My friend made no reply, but wobbled slightly as he tried to stop the spinning of his head. I somehow expected him to appear unfazed by the ordeal. He was perfectly built for this type of daily grind. Suddenly a thought crossed my mind and I began to laugh. My friend took the gesture as a sign that the spirit approved of his offering of the mammoth. I put my hand on the primitive man's shoulder.

"Since I feel like Robinson Caruso, I might as well call you by the name, 'Friday'." The other man took my smile in good will, and smiled back at me. For a brief second, I could see the hole where once stood Friday's plagued tooth. I looked at the space for a moment, and then began to laugh even harder.

"I am the first Dentist."

Friday noticed that my nose was no longer red, but black and blue, and he too burst out laughing. It had been the first time that I had heard him vocalize anything close to what I considered to be recognizable human sounds, and the laughter quickly died as I reflected on just how advanced this man might be. Friday felt my mood of uncertainty, and unceremoniously walked over to the slain body. I in turn, studied him as he walked away. This was a Neanderthal, a so-called primitive man. Yet he walked upright, was more muscular than I was, he could move with greater agility, and seemed to be very intelligent. I had read that the current anthropological theories all lead to these same conclusions, but with all the past years of being stereotyped with inaccurate information, such as Neanderthals being primitive or down right unintelligent, I found it difficult to believe my eyes. Why this race would come to die out, I would never know. They could survive in the harshest environment better than modern man, so the reason had to lie elsewhere. Then it occurred to me, Friday had not yet spoken a word, let alone a complete sentence. Maybe this was what led to eventual downfall.

As I walked over to the mammoth, I saw Friday pull a leather bag out from under his over-hanging fur garment. He placed the bag on the ground, and began to meticulously unwrap it. I peered over his shoulder and watched as Friday was hunched over and down on his knees selecting several fine bladed obsidian tools.

"Looks like something I saw in Scientific American." Friday was undaunted by my words, and with a stone blade he began slicing around the mammoth's heavily folded neck.

"Hold it," I pulled back on Friday's shoulder and it looked like he was ready to fight off an attack.

"Try using this," in rapid succession I pulled out my knife, flicked the blade open, and cut into the Mammoth's meat. He watched with great fascination. I handed him the knife by the handle end. Friday took the knife, and without any forethought, began to use it deafly on the tough hide, with immediate improved results.

"You're flint blade is technically sharper than surgical steel, but my blade is longer. Oh, you can get one at any Sears store, and Craftsman tools are guaranteed for life, but I'm not sure if prehistory life counts."

Friday smiled at me, almost as if he understood what I was saying, and then proceeded to speak. He began by rattling off a series of vowels and consonants intermixed with deep guttural intonations.

"I froze and stared at him in amazement. Why did he remain silent until now? My mind raced for possible explanations, but found none. Friday continued working skillfully, tearing the hide away from the animal's body. Following a specific sequence of movements, he had peeled off the fur, down to the ankle joints, and was now lifting the massive piece of skin over the mammoth's back. This was as much as he could do without having to turn over the eight-ton carcass. Friday then ignored the fur and busily went to work at cutting the meat into long strips. He kept on talking through the entire process, but I noticed that every once in a while, he would take time out to take his hand and touch the area on his mouth where the tooth had once infested while he listened and looked around. That must be what kept him from talking, I figured out. Until now, he must have been in too much pain to even attempt speaking. However, with the advent of speech, I could see even fewer reasons for Friday's race to die out.

"I bet the aliens caused your race to vanish." I said. Friday looked over at me and cocked his head as if he understood every word.

"Of course, if they can put me here, then they certainly could have wiped your race out of existence. I would be willing to bet that they used your kind for so-called scientific studies. Like the Nazis did in World War Two". I glanced up at the sky, and Friday looked up as well, but as expected, Friday could not see what I, the spirit could see.

"I swear that if I ever meet the aliens again, I will kill each and everyone of them. We are not guinea pigs to be played and experimented with, we are humans!" Friday did not know what my hand gestures meant, but he saw a small dire wolf moving near the far tree line and he immediately went back to work, at an even faster pace than before. I did not see the wolf until it had come a considerable degree closer to our kill. The wolf was small, mostly white in color with several black patches running along the sides of its body. Although the animal was almost starving, she kept her distance from us. Friday stopped cutting strips of meat and instead started pulling back the exposed hide away from the main body of the mammoth. I did not know why Friday was working so hard, nor did I even know how to offer any help. All I could do was watch and listen to Friday as he began to chant.

"I sure wish I knew what you were saying." Friday abruptly stopped his chant, slung several pieces of meat over his shoulder, stood up, and after handing me back my knife he began marching off over the short hillside to his old campsite. There was nothing for me to do, but follow. Reaching the campsite, he dropped the meat to the ground next to the fire pit that was still smoldering. He threw some small dried tinder on the coals and marched back towards the mammoth. This time I knew what Friday was going to do so I handed back my knife to him, so after Friday had cut some more pieces of flesh he put them over his shoulder, I cut a few long strips of meat and put them over my shoulder. Friday was shocked at first, but the help was greatly needed. It was impossible for me to carry as much meat as Friday though.

"I may not be as strong as you Friday, but I think we could still make a great team." Friday saw irrepressible smile, and he could not help but do the same. The spirit was pleased with him, Friday thought, and had even offered to share in his workload. Maybe the spirit would let him live and not kill him one tooth at a time.

As we returned to the scene of the Mammoth carcass, I caught sight of the wolf chewing on the meat. Upon spotting us, the wolf quickly stopped trying to tear off a piece of meat and moved off to a relatively safe distance. Reaching the carcass, I cut off a good-sized piece of meat, and tossed it in the general direction of the wolf. The creature at once lunged at the piece of meat and carried it off to eat at a safer location.

"That is man's future best friend." Friday did not understand my actions and looked at me as if I lost my mind.

"Now we won't be bothered by her any longer."

Together we hauled an entire leg and a portion of the hip, over to the campsite. When we arrived back to the now burning fire, I was exhausted. I would have liked to take a break, but the minute Friday let go of his load, he was once again heading back towards the mammoth.

"What's the rush?" I yelled out, but Friday appeared to ignore me. I noticed the blood covering his suit, and I decided that it was time to take a break with or without him to wash off the filthy mess. Standing down by the edge of the lake, I saw Friday carrying two more chunks of meat hung over his spear, and a large section of ribs tucked tightly under his arm. He still had not slowed down. The man was an unstoppable beast. As far as I was concerned, the meat could wait awhile before I was going to do any more hauling. I was out of shape and my neck already felt sore from the lifting I had done so far. After washing off most of the blood, I stood and stared into the lake. A group of birds taking to flight from a far off forested area finally broke my moment of peace, and I started up the ridge towards the mammoth. When I arrived, I found a bloody mess with Friday standing in the middle. He was making the last cuts with his tools that would release a large portion of hide away from the rest of the half butchered carcass. Only the head, feet and tusks remained exempt from his fleecing instruments. Scraping away at the last few strips of clinging meat and fat, Friday began to pull the heavy piece of fur away from the rest of the carcass. Without thinking, I reached down, grasped the hide with both hands, and helped pull the fur out from under the huge clutter of flesh and bones. Friday kept pulling on the fur even after it had been cleared away from the rest of the pile. It was soon obvious that he intended to drag the fur down to the lake. I noticed his Fridays spear lying in the middle of the fur, so as we passed the spear I made, I too threw my spear in with his, and once again helped lug the heavy carpet of skin.

Down at the lake, Friday washed the hide and removed most of the blood. Then he dragged the hide back to the campsite, meanwhile the dragging parts collected mud and debris along the way. Having draped the fur over a large rock, he left the campsite again. This time, however, he headed off in a different direction. I reluctantly followed.

"Oh, so your collecting firewood," I said to him as I watched him grabbing at all the wood in sight. It didn't seem to bother Friday which wood was wet and which pieces were dry, it only mattered which pieces were the easiest to collect. On the other hand, Friday kept and eye on me and had a puzzled look on his face as I meticulously gathered only the driest pieces. I noticed the expression on his friends face.

"Don't worry, it will all make sense to you in another five thousand years or so." The sun was getting low in the sky. Today was a good day, I thought. I could feel the sun's rays from time to time as the overhead clouds randomly drifted apart. Sitting with my back against a rock, I diligently watched as Friday tried to start a fire. Using a bowed piece of wood between his hands, he rubbed his hands back and forth in hopes of igniting a small cluster of dried grass. I thought that the entire procedure was a waste of time, but as I was about to vocalize this point to Friday, the clump of dried grass ignited. Much to Friday's credit, he picked through all the wood he collected and only selected the dry wood to place on the burgeoning fire first. Soon a giant pile of wood was blazing almost out of control. I had to move back several feet as the fire reached its peak. Suddenly, over the roar of the fire, I heard the roar of a bear, probably the one I had seen earlier. I then realized why the fire had to be so big.

"Yeah, you knew that he would show up all along, didn't you?" But there was no answer from Friday, as he busily placed the strips of meat on top of sticks stuck in the ground that were standing near the fire.

"That's why you were moving so fast too." Friday still ignored me and continued setting up the stakes of meat. It would take at least two days for the meat to become dry enough to prevent spoilage. By then, the bear would once again be on the prowl, but until that time, the remains of mammoth's carcass would keep it and other predators satisfied. The rest of the evening, the two of us snacked on charcoaled smoked ribs, while I watched Friday carve the remainder of the meat into small enough strips to hang on sticks for drying. I thought that the meat was tasty, but even if I could have had ketchup or I still would have rather been eating at McDonald's, Burger King, Wendy's or my favorite Taco Bell. I began thinking about the fast food withdrawals that I was going to have to endure. These thoughts alone almost brought pain to my stomach.

PAGE 300

As night fell, the fire was still burning brightly. Several hours had
passed since we had last heard the bear's roar, but we knew that he
was still close by. The winds had died down considerably from the
previous night. Lying on the ground, close to the fire, I stared into
the flames as my body absorbed the gradient heat, occasionally
averting my eyes to watch Friday get up from his resting position
to feed the fire another log. I contemplated his situation, and while
gazing into the reddish-orange colored coals, several questions
entered my mind. Those that were not as important faded quickly
to make room for the questions that bothered me the most. Soon
all thoughts fled, as I could no longer keep my eyes open to watch
the burning embers. Early in the morning, Friday woke up and
began collecting more wood, while I tried to sleep some more.
After returning, he piled the wood high on top of the fire. Soon the
flames had increased their heat to the point that I could barely
tolerate the heat. My body wanted to move away from the blaze as
he entered a restless dream state. Visions of Friday and me
marching along mountain ridges passed through my head. Our
journeys would lead us to encounter all types of creatures that had
long since vanished from the face of the Earth. Some animals were
even from the wrong age in time, but it was not the animals
themselves that mattered, just the thoughts of trying to deal with
objects from the past, and in all situations, I felt totally helpless in
dealing with my surroundings. After awhile, Friday entered my
dream again, and lead me down to a village that lay at the base of a
cliff. Small huts made of grass could be seen with more people of
Friday's own race peeking at me from behind rocks and walls of
their shelters. On the face of the cliff, a large opening lead inside a
cave. Several broad shouldered Neanderthal men stood at the
opening, and watched as we approached. The men were all dressed
in long furred garments, similar to one that Friday wore. One of the
men in the middle had a necklace around his neck. It was tooth-
laced with large wild animal canines. Friday stopped a few feet in
front of the one with the adornment, and I followed his lead. The
rest of the men looked to their necklace-laden chief to see what

would happen next. He studied me for a moment, and then signaled for Friday to speak. Some how Friday's face was no longer swollen and he immediately opened up by telling a long tale with words and the use of his hands. I could almost understand all of what was being told, for the graphic body gestures that accompanied the speech were very explicit. Especially about discovering the location of a herd of mammoths and the tooth. The chief listened intently to the speech, and when Friday finished, he abruptly turned away and headed back into the cave. The rest of his men followed close behind. They stood there for nearly half an hour before the chief marched back out of the cave. When he did, he placed his arms around Friday, and welcomed him back to the village. Releasing his embrace from his fellow man, he then turned and embraced me. I was then escorted inside the cave to sit before an open bed of coals. In my dream, I was no longer wearing my moon suit. I was now dressed in furs like the others. A group of ten, we sat around the fire with knees crossed and passed a large piece of bone that had been carved into a shallow bowl. Each of the men sipped from the bowl and then passed it on. I looked into the depths of the bow, but the cave was so dark, that I could only see the reflection of the fire on the surface of the liquid. The contents of the bowl would remain a mystery to my eyes. I took a sip of broth; it was lukewarm and had a very tart flavor. Letting the liquid slide down the back of my throat caused my throat to burn. By the time the uncomfortable sensation stopped, the bowl had been passed around, and it was once again my turn. The bowl was as full as I last looked into it. After having several sips of the drink, I began to feel disoriented. Soon, I felt the lifting of my body by several of the surrounding men, and I was carried out of the cave and into one of the nearby grass huts. Dropping my body onto a pile of multicolored furs, the men left and I was alone. Gazing at the ceiling I wondered what would happen next. I didn't have to wonder long, for into the hut walked a woman.

The face seemed familiar, but I just couldn't place it. Then suddenly, I remembered, the woman was Julie. I tried to rise up off the floor and ask her why she was not at Expom, and why she was here, but the words came out slurred, and my head was too dizzy to rise. Julie remained silent as she lay down next to me. I closed my eyes for a fraction of a second, and when I opened my eyes, I was startled to find that the woman lying next to me was not Julie, but one of the Neanderthal women. Quickly I got up and wanted to shout out, but could only clear my throat, which had become burned by the strange elixir.

The woman became frightened of me and went to the far corner of the hut. Two men entered the hut and pinned me to the floor. I cursed at them, as I tried to break their grip on me, but my struggle was in vain. Then as I quieted down, the woman began to scream as her stomach enlarged. I once again struggled to be free as I starred at the woman. To my amazement she was becoming more pregnant by the second. Two women rushed into the hut, and soon the woman was going into labor. I froze in terror as I found myself witnessing the birth. A baby began to emerge from out of the womb, with features that were without a doubt closer to my own than their race. I watched as the chief raised the baby high into the air by its tiny feet and talked in praise. Then suddenly, the chief looked over at me, pointed his finger, and then I felt a piercing pain in my chest.

Turns out, the pain was real, but from the spear of Friday. I woke out of my sleep to the voice of Friday. He had heard me cursing and screaming as he was gathering more wood, and had just momentarily arrived to see what had happened. He must have thought I was crazy, yet he had no idea as to what had caused a sleeping man to be this way, so he stopped poking me and backed away and sat down in fear of what he didn't understand, with his spear still pointed towards me.

When I finally woke up enough to become aware of my actions, I looked at Friday and smiled.

"Nothing to be afraid of." I could see the concern on his face. I reached for a piece of meat hung over the end of one of the steaks, and as I began chewing my breakfast, I thought about what significance the dream could have in my future. It wasn't that I believed that dreams could come true; it was just that this one seemed so real that it surely had to have some foreboding meaning. Entering the village, having sex with one of them, and then being killed. As I finished my summation, it finally dawned on me why I was left here. I was not left behind to teach and educate, but merely to combine my genetic pool with a race of primitive people in order to speed up evolution. If I died or not, seemed to be of little concern to the aliens and whether or not I passed on my genes, did not interest me in the least. All I wanted to do at this point was to stay alive until I could get revenge for what the aliens had done to me. They had no right interfering with humans or anything else for that matter, and I was determined to bring this point to their attention.

However, in the meantime, I would have to survive with the help of Friday and the rest of his race for the rest of history. No, I take that back. I would not help Friday's race exist. That kind of plan never worked out. Friday's race for no known reason to me would fall short by the roll of the dice. They would do no better that the bow and arrow wielding first nations hunter-gatherers did against the gun wielding colonists or the Incas and Mayans did against the sword yielding horsemen of Spain. They needed more than my knowledge of science and art. What they needed was a jumpstart to civilization. Then it came to me, Neanderthals had never formed in groups larger than clans and villages. If I could turn them into an empire, before my own race came to dominate, it could turn the cards on which species came to dominate this part of the world. The aliens would find themselves forced to come back in time after me before I turned history on it's head. I would start with agriculture and turn Neanderthals into farmers with more food than they could ever use. I would show them how to make weapons and tools forged from standing hearths using fire, coal, and whatever metals deposits we found. I could advance their living conditions; teach them about sanitation, health, and medicine. Neanderthals would become the greatest race on the planet. I could turn them into the greatest warriors ever and I would set traps for the aliens so when they returned to reverse or impede my progress, it would cost them dearly. Life was looking good. It was time to rewrite history…right after I taught them how to write that is.

Epilogue

Jason placed the last page of the manuscript neatly back down in the box. He had been up reading the manuscript until he finished it and the digital clock on his dresser read 3am. He had been a speed-reader since his freshman year in high school, but this work took longer to read because his mind often drifted to other worlds when he read science fiction. The story seemed generic enough to almost not be worth reading. It could have been written last week by the appearance of the text and scientific accuracy of the moon, but his grandfather said it was written a while back, and the paper looked as old as his grandfather. So why take the time to make the manuscript look typed by an out of date typewriter on paper old as the Egyptians? Perhaps when he asked his grandfather what happened to the first twenty two pages it would all make sense. Jason turned out the light and fell fast asleep.

In the morning he woke up in the middle of a dream where he was stranded alone on the moon. He got right out of bed and took a quick shower and then caught a bus going down by his grandfather's apartment building. His grandfather was already out on the porch and his face lit up into a big bright smile as he saw his grandson walking towards him.

"Hello Jason, sleep well?"

"No, Grandpa,"

"What seems to be the matter?"

"That manuscript. I read the whole thing last night. Parts of it seemed real, and parts were definitely made up, but I liked the part about the tennis guy being named Jason. Is that how I got my name?"

"Oh, you would have to ask your father about that. I personally used that manuscript as a tool for investment."

"What do you mean, Grandpa?"

"I invested in anything and everything that had to do with space, ceramic materials, Taco Bell, Burger King and even Gore-tex. That's how I made my money."

"Anyone, could have done that without this story."

"I guess, but the book gave me vision and incentive. The manuscript was the vision, and pressed in the middle of the pages was this." His grandfather opened his hand and revealed a slightly elongated tooth. Jason's eyes got wide and he shook his head.

"No, that can't be..."

"Oh, but it is. I had some university friends check it out. It's the exact tooth shape of a Neanderthal's at less than thirty years of age, but it's less than one hundred years old. Only one problem though, it contains Carbon14 levels well below anything born and living after1945 when hydrogen bombs elevated C14 atmospheric levels, so it can't be a tooth from any recently living human, but it's not old enough to be a fossil either."

"So why show me Grandpa?"

"All I am saying is, study hard in school, use the manuscript for insights into investments, and in about twenty some years you could be that tennis player on the moon."

"And if I don't?"

"Hey, perhaps Expom will never exist, but if it does, you can't go there unless you are prepared for it. A good degree in mechanical engineering might come in handy too."

"You could say that about anything in life, Grandpa." His grandpa handed him the tooth.

"That you can son, and that's what makes everything including this book possible."

"So what happened to the guy who wrote this?"

"Dr. Wilson? Died in the fire I suppose. It was either his time to go or it was made to look like his time go. I never wanted to go there, because the man wasn't right in the head."

"Because he was trying to change history?"

"Because he was trying to play in the big leagues, and the aliens are in a league of their own."

"So you think the aliens are real?"

"As real as that tooth."

THE END

www.ingramcontent.com/pod-product-compliance
Lightning Source LLC
Chambersburg PA
CBHW070918130626
46555CB00001B/185